THE GREEN PARAKEETS

THE GREEN PARAKEETS

Hilary Wilde

CHIVERS

British Library Cataloguing in Publication Data available

This Large Print edition published by AudioGO Ltd, Bath, 2012.
Published by arrangement with the Author's Estate

U.K. Hardcover   ISBN 978 1 4713 0634 1
U.K. Softcover   ISBN 978 1 4713 0635 8

Printed and bound in Great Britain by
MPG Books Group Limited

CHAPTER ONE

Annette had gone to the bathroom to fetch her father's medicine when she heard the sound of a horse's hooves. Looking out of the window, she saw that a man was riding down the lane towards the house. Although she had not yet met him, she knew instantly that it could only be 'Himself', as the Islanders called the Seigneur, Henri Revoir.

Annette hid behind the pink curtains, not wanting him to see her, yet curious herself to know what this strange man was like. She had heard so much about him in the ten days she had been on this fabulous island set in the Indian Ocean.

Henri Revoir was fabulous too, she thought, as she watched the black horse walk with slow stately steps down the lane under the green trees which met overhead under a blue cloudless sky. This tall man in the white riding breeches, shining boots, white silk shirt and bare head was an impressive-looking person. Like his father before him, he defied the sun and refused to wear a hat. But, unlike his father, he had copper-red hair.

That was one of the things the French Islanders had against him. Who had ever heard of a Frenchman, they said, with red hair? But the Seigneur was not all French. Like Annette,

1

he was half and half. His mother was English but his father was French—whereas Annette's mother had been French and her father was English.

It was sad that the Islanders disliked 'Himself, so much. They said that red hair meant a bad temper and, indeed, was it not true? How often he was very angry, impatient and intolerant! Rumour had it that, since he had inherited the Island, he had openly admitted that he disliked everything about it and the people, and had thought of selling the place. What a terrible thing for him to have said! Had the Revoirs not been there since the beginning of the nineteenth century? Were not the very Creoles on the estate descendants of the first slaves that the first Henri Revoir had brought out with him?

As Annette watched him, the man rode down towards the little house slowly. Her awe mounted as she saw him more clearly, and she understood why so many people feared him. She even shivered a little at the thought of ever finding herself facing his anger. Yet how good-looking he was. Never in all her eighteen years had she seen such a handsome, impressive-looking man.

She watched a tiny red bird as it flashed past the open window and dived into a bush of pink aloes. Oh, how colourful and lovely the Island was—how different from the village in Somerset that had been all she had ever known of the world before.

'Himself' was getting closer now. How easily he rode. How magnificent he looked. Truly, she could imagine him riding into battle in the olden days—so dashing, so courageous. He must be a tall man, she reflected. How odd that the Islanders should have christened Henri Revoir 'Himself'. Madame Casca, the friendly little Frenchwoman who lived down the hill, had laughed when Annette spoke about this and asked her: 'What *can* we call him?'

Of course there was a legend about the Revoirs—there were legends about everything on the Island. This Henry Revoir—for he used the English version of his name—was the second son of the Henri Revoir of Resistance fame and the son of Henri's second wife who had been an Englishwoman, hating the Island, refusing to live on it.

Henri Revoir had been known as *le Colonel;* his first-born son, the son of a Frenchwoman and whose name was Maurice, had been *le Capitaine.* Both had fought valiantly for France in the underground movement. Henry, however, had been a schoolboy in England when war was declared and had been rushed to the safety of America by his devoted mother, there to finish his education. He had no war service, it was said. Annette wondered why—he could not have been delicate. He must have been too young. That meant then that he must

3

be younger than he looked.

It was because of the war that Annette's father, Randal Laleham, and Henri Revoir—*le Colonel*—had become friends and comrades. Randal, happily married to a Frenchwoman, had invested all his money in France, had settled there and had fought side by side with the French. First he sent his French wife and their tiny baby to England and it was not until Annette was five years old that she saw him again. By then, her mother was dead. After a long cold winter, she had died of pneumonia, according to the doctor.

It was the first Randal had known of it and, even although Annette had been so young, she could remember his shattered look, his long silences, and although he made a great fuss of his little daughter he had neither stayed in England with her nor taken her away with him. He had left Annette with 'Aunt' Maggie, an old friend of the family who ran a girls' boarding school in the country village, and he had written long intimate letters to his daughter through the years, letters that were like hands of love stretched across the thousands of miles that separated them, but never once had he suggested that his daughter should live with him.

This had always hurt Annette; she had torn up so many letters she had written in which she begged him to let her join him, but always hesitated to post them, afraid lest he did not want her, believing that he was happier travelling round the world alone, or living in places where it was not suitable for a young girl to be.

That was why his cable had been so wonderful. Just a few weeks earlier it had arrived, instructing her to fly out at once, saying all arrangements had been made through the local bank; the same bank to which he sent, every month, her allowance. How thrilled she had been.

Now she hastily pulled across the curtains, luckily finding a small hole in the material through which she could peep as 'Himself' passed by, so close she could see the colour of his eyes—green with strange golden streaks. The parakeets chose that moment to screech angrily from their perches in the feathery casuarina trees. It was odd how they seemed to hate visitors . . .

Was 'Himself' going to be a visitor? Now he seemed to be looking directly at Annette and she shrank back, afraid he could see her. She sighed with a mixture of relief and disappointment as he rode by, going on down the lane which dropped so steeply down the hill towards a few campments, before ending abruptly on the sands and the rugged rocks against which the ocean rollers pounded incessantly. Those same rollers that shook the cliff on which this small house was built, causing it to shake with a regular rhythm that in time one hardly noticed, for there was always the roar of the ocean to make a background to one's conversation or thoughts.

'Himself' would have to return this way, for the road led nowhere. Would he visit them then? It seemed likely. Her father had often wondered why Henry had not called already, for naturally he would want to meet her.

'He is a good man,' Annette's father was always saying. 'A fine man—a man to respect.'

It was odd, but the qualities her father approved of in Henry Revoir were the very ones of which the Cascas disapproved. Madame Casca was the most tolerant and sometimes admitted that 'Himself' had some good points. It must be hard to face such hostility, Annette thought, as she hurried to her bedroom, looking ruefully down at her faded cotton frock, her bare legs and old sandals. She would not like the Seigneur to see her looking like this!

She loved the little house. It was beautifully furnished with very good antique furniture. It was shabby, but nothing shoddy. Pierre, the huge Creole who waited so attentively on her invalid father, was not very good at housework. Like all Creoles he was born lazy, her father said tolerantly. But Pierre more than made up for this by the gentle way he carried her paralysed parent from his bed to the wicker lounge chair on the veranda and then back to the couch in the sitting-room, bathing, dressing, even scolding him when necessary. Such devotion was rare.

What a shock it had been when she arrived to find that her father had completely lost the use of his legs. He had never mentioned illness. When she told Madame Casca this, the Frenchwoman had shown no surprise.

'Your father is a proud man, he feared compassion,' she said.

Annette opened her wardrobe door and gazed within. She had practically nothing to wear, for she had taken the very minimum of clothing when she flew out, not knowing if she was to stay with her father permanently. Now she gave a quick, fervent prayer that she would not be sent away. How could she bear to leave him? To return to that small narrow village, the busy days, the absence of love . . .

Washing quickly, she thought that it was love she had always missed. Aunt Maggie had been kind but impersonal and nothing had ever replaced the warm demonstrative love Annette's own mother had shown. Nor had it ever been the same as the love her father showed every time he smiled at her. If only . . . if only he had sent for her before!

As she sat on the brass-railed bedstead and put on her only good pair of nylon stockings, she thought she would ask Madame Casca to tell her why her father had never sent for her before, and if there was a chance that she could stay for good.

She slid into the turquoise blue sheath frock that she had just finished making when that exciting, unbelievable cable had arrived. She had dropped everything, rushing off on her bicycle to the market town and the bank, there to meet the manager for the first time because Aunt Maggie had always collected her allowance. Annette had been afraid it was a dream. But no—it was true! Her father *had* sent for her.

She drew her wide belt tightly round her narrow waist. How lucky she was not to have to bother about puppy fat, for when you are only five feet two inches tall, you dare not be plump!

Brushing her short curly dark hair with vigorous strokes, she examined her face in the mirror, then hurried to the bathroom to dampen her fringe and twist it into small curls. What sort of man was Henry Revoir? What would he think of her? He was the kind who would be difficult to please, the kind every woman would want to impress. If only she did not look so terribly young; even though her mouth was a sophisticated scarlet and her dark hair gleamed, she still looked very youthful.

Remembering her father's medicine, she was full of apologies as she took it to him on the veranda. 'I am sorry,' she said lovingly.

He held out his thin white hand as she pulled a pouffe close to his side and sat there smiling at him, trying to hide the anxiety she

8

felt.

Waiting for him to swallow his unpalatable medicine, she looked over the low wall of the veranda and at the deep sapphire blue sea and the huge waves that raced towards the land. It was all so incredibly lovely; that sky with not a cloud to disturb its blueness, the distant mountains that shimmered in the heat on the other side of the wide bay; and the trees, tall and straight, whose trunks and branches were decorated with the stems and purple trumpet flowers called Morning Glory. She could watch the birds for hours—look at that beautiful honey-bird with his small scarlet chest and blue wings as he hovered over a flower, his long, curved beak ready to be thrust deep into the heart of the flower to seek the nectar.

'You look just like your mother,' her father said abruptly.

Annette turned, took the empty glass and smiled. 'Am I like her?'

He took her hand. 'So very like her. She was your age when we met.' He closed his eyes and said tenderly, 'So lovely, so young and so naïve. She had your soft dark hair, your strange eyes and sweet mouth—your nature.' He looked at her and she saw fear in his eyes for a moment. 'You must choose your husband wisely, my little Annette. Women like you and your mother are so easily hurt.'

'I shan't marry for ages,' she told him, clinging to his hand. 'I—I've not thought of it.'

Her father sighed. 'Sometimes we must think of these things without warning. Choose a kind man, my darling. I only wish—' He stopped speaking and hesitated, still looking at her. He touched her frock and smiled, his voice changing. 'And for whom is all this splendour?' he teased.

Annette felt her cheeks go hot. 'I saw "Himself" ride by and thought he might look in on his way back,' she admitted.

'I wish you wouldn't call him that,' her father said in a sad voice. 'He is a fine man. It is unfortunate that he has upset the Islanders. It is not his fault. Remember that they are a queer lot, my child—feudal and loyal, but oh, so narrow-minded. They are lazy with the laziness of years of dependence.

'It is not Henry's fault that he is more English than French, that this sort of life is alien to him or that he looks at every problem from a different angle. He has been very good to me, Annette, like his father before him. He is a generous man and ashamed lest his generosity be termed weakness—or his kindness cause dependence.' He closed his eyes and Annette watched him worriedly, for he grew tired so very easily.

Sitting quietly, she looked through the open archway that led to the house; all the doors were open to invite every small breath of air for the heat was terrific. A pretty house it was, and an enchanting island. She thought of the

10

day she had arrived, flying out from England, changing into a smaller plane at Mauritius to bring her to the Island Revoir. How eagerly she had looked out, how disappointed when her father was not there to meet her. But a cream car with a Creole chauffeur had been sent to fetch her and had whisked her away from the plane through a village which seemed to be a long stretch of small houses, mostly rose red, with shingled green roofs and white shutters. The street was crowded and the car had to weave its way through a strange assortment, coolies pulling two-wheeled rickshaws, a crowd of people with different coloured skins, strange clothes, bright beady eyes turning to stare at her. There were small buildings with turrets that looked very white in the sunshine, shadowed, sinister-looking alleys, always people.

It was a swift passage past the strange faces and she was eager to reach her father's side, so she only had a confused impression of seeing a group of monks in their black habits with huge white topees on their heads; some Chinese, their hands hidden in wide sleeves; a nun with a chocolate brown serene face and a lot of natives, coffee brown in colour, huge white cloaks hiding their bodies, on their heads wide raffia-woven hats.

Annette had not been back to the village, for in the ten days since her arrival, she had stayed close to her father, only visiting

11

the Cascas. Madame Casca had been with Annette's father when she arrived, had taken the tired, frightened girl to her plump bosom, kissing her first on one cheek and then on the other, exclaiming aloud in delight when Annette spoke in her easy colloquial French.

'Alors—c'est impossible—an English girl and she speaks our tongue so prettily.'

Annette had smiled shyly at her father, trying to recognize some familiar feature in the thin pale face. But at five years of age you notice little and remember less. Even then, he had been thin and white, recently released from a prisoner of war camp.

'I am glad you have kept up your French,' he said in a stiff voice.

Annette had known that he, too, was shy. It had been so long—too long.

'In our village there was an elderly couple, refugees from France. Often I visited them. They taught me to think in French. Always it brought *maman* close to me when I spoke French,' she explained.

'C'est magnzfique. Quel plaisir,' Madame Casca cried, and ever since then, Annette had talked to the Cascas only in French; yet oddly enough she felt more at ease with her father if she talked English to him

Suddenly the quiet air was split by the angry screeching of the parakeets. Her father opened his eyes and smiled.

'Our visitor, I think,' he said.

12

Annette was on her feet, her hand flying nervously to her hair as Pierre, his heavy fleshy face impassive, his dark eyes intent on his master's face, came padding in, his feet bare and his white suit crumpled as if he had slept in it.

'The Seigneur,' he announced in his deep growl, gave a bow and backed away.

'Himself' stood in the doorway. He was staring at her. Oh, he was quite, quite something—or rather someone, she thought with a breathless feeling. How tall he was. He kept staring at her. Was her nose red? Had her fringe gone straight—were her stocking seams all right? She resisted the desire to look in the mirror on the wall, and moved forward, awkwardly, self-consciously, so that the high heel of her shoe twisted in the rug and she went plunging forward.

Henry Revoir caught her, held her for a breathtaking moment, and then steadied her on her feet and released her. She apologized, feeling her face was on fire. He gave her a very brief smile and then looked over her head at her father.

'And how are you, Mr. Laleham?' he asked as he took the invalid's thin white hand in his tanned one. 'I would have come before, but things have been a little difficult,' he said apologetically.

'You will convince them in time,' Randal Laleham said, his voice surprisingly strong for a moment.

'But have I enough time?' Henry Revoir asked slowly. He turned to look at Annette. 'And so this is your little daughter. She is not like you.'

'Thanks be,' Randal Laleham said with a smile. 'No, she is exactly like her mother, a born Frenchwoman,' he said proudly.

'Himself' was frowning. Now she could see that not only was he very good-looking but there seemed not a single thing wrong in that perfect face. Oh yes, there was—one—a silly little thing. He had a small brown mole under his right ear. It looked out of place on that smooth, sun-tanned skin with his perfectly even white teeth and straight nose.

'But I understood your daughter has lived all her life in England,' Henry Revoir said thoughtfully.

'I have,' Annette told him quickly, for already her father was looking tired. 'My mother was French and I loved the language.'

'You speak French well?' Henry said.

Was it right that a man should have such long lashes? Look how they rested on his cheek when he closed his eyes. Fair lashes, tipped with gold.

'And what do you think of the Island?' he asked, opening his eyes, giving her that shrewd thoughtful look she found rather alarming.

'I—I love it,' she stammered a little. 'It's so beautiful.'

14

'First impressions. You'd soon get bored here. Nothing to do, always so hot. Wait until the cyclone season starts,' Henry said, sounding amused.

For a moment she temporarily lost her awe of him and knew only anger. Did he want her to leave Revoir Island? Her father was looking quite worried. Oh, why must 'Himself' be so thoughtless—or was it deliberately unkind? He must know she wanted to stay with her father, yet he was trying to spoil things, to make her father think she would not be happy here.

'I'm never bored,' she said, almost violently. 'It couldn't be too hot for me, and I don't believe you have cyclones.' She finished rather abruptly, for now Henry was smiling at her— the tolerant smile of an adult for a rebellious, foolish child.

'Wait and see,' he said dryly, and then turned to her father.

'I'd like to talk business with you, Mr. Laleham. Could your daughter—'

Annette caught her breath, lifted her head and her small, firm chin. 'I will visit my friends,' she told him haughtily. Then she hesitated, looking worriedly at her father and then tilting back her head to stare up at the tall, handsome man who was surveying her with such impatience and an obvious desire to see the back of her. 'My father gets easily tired.'

Henry Revoir's hand was on her arm and he

was turning her towards the archway. 'I wasn't born yesterday,' he assured her. 'And be careful you don't sprain your ankle with those ridiculous heels.'

She was being slowly but firmly hustled along.

She spoke over her shoulder angrily. 'They're not ridiculous.'

'They are—when you are obviously not used to them,' he retorted as he released her shoulder and left her, the amusement in his voice still ringing in her ears.

She felt depressed as she went to her bedroom and meekly changed her shoes. He was the sort of man who would always be right. For a moment she hated him violently. How dare he treat her as a child? Why, he had not even noticed that she was wearing her prettiest frock. He was not the slightest bit—not the tiniest, weeniest little bit—interested in her. In fact, she doubted very much if he had seen her at all, for all that rude staring of his. Her eyes stung as she hurried. At least the Cascas liked her. They 'saw' her all right, particularly Jean Casca, an extremely attractive young man!

CHAPTER TWO

Twenty minutes later she was on her way down the hill, past the eucalyptus trees, past the flamboyants and the group of three coco-palms which stood, bending away from the sea, and shivering a little in the welcome breeze that had sprung up. Wearing a shady hat and dark glasses, Annette gave a little skip of happiness as she thought of the pleasant hour that lay ahead of her. She would not hurry home. Then 'Himself' might have gone. She did not want to see him again!

She opened the white gate that led to the Cascas' villa just as two yellow birds darted out of the bushes and brushed past her face.

The front door, its paint cracked and peeling from the heat of the sun, was ajar as usual and when she called gently, Madame Lucille Casca came hurrying down the paved hall to meet her. Madame's face was bright with pleasure as she cradled Annette in her arms for a moment, her bright red lips lightly touching Annette's cheeks.

'*Quel plaisir,*' Madame cried delightedly.

Annette was seated in a deep chair on the veranda, facing the sea. From this level she could see how huge were the racing rollers as they came bounding in to break into fragments of rainbow-hued glory on the rocks. The roar was much louder down here nearer the water.

Jean Casca and his sister were both on the veranda and Jean had risen to his feet to greet Annette. A tall, dark-haired young man with twinkling mischievous eyes and a small moustache, he bent over her hand and kissed it so naturally that it was impossible to feel embarrassed.

'Enchanté,' he murmured, and went back to the easel before which he had been sitting. He picked up his brush and started to paint. 'You will excuse?' he asked.

Madeleine, his sister, was stretched out on a *chaise-longue,* lovely in an old-gold coloured silk frock. She lifted a friendly pink-tipped hand in lazy greeting but did not move her position. Her head was resting on one hand, her face turned plaintively towards Jean. Annette stared at her in admiration. How very lovely she was with a skin like a magnolia petal, that long dark gleaming hair twisted into an apparently careless knot, her long, slim body the very essence of grace.

'Will you paint me one day, Jean?' Annette asked. She crossed her fingers quickly, for it seemed like tempting fate. Dare she hope to stay with her father for ever?

Jean looked up and his face was bright with laughter. 'When you grow up, *petit choux,*' he said teasingly.

'I am grown up,' Annette began indignantly.

Jean looked at her and ran a finger slowly

18

along his moustache as if to hide a smile. 'But you have not suffered yet, my child,' he told her lazily.

'Has Mad—' Annette began, but the words died away and her cheeks were hot. 'I'm sorry, Madeleine,' she apologized. 'I forgot.'

Madeleine was smiling at her. 'Do not fear—it is passing. Already that terrible sorrow is more bearable. One day it will have quite gone,' she said.

'I do hope so,' Annette said fervently. She knew very little about Madeleine's tragedy— simply that she had loved and lost someone, but sometimes Jean would tease his sister and then Madeleine's fury would dissolve in bitter tears and self-recriminations about what she should have done—what she might have done—if only.

As Annette looked round her, she unconsciously relaxed, for here in this household she was always at ease. There was such a 'comfortable' atmosphere here. No one quarrelled, or only rarely; no one worked very hard or worried about anything. They all seemed to believe that 'the Lord will provide', though Annette's father said he thought they often mistook the Revoir family for the Lord and expected miracles!

The villa was not large, and yet with its big windows and wide open doors it gave an illusion of space. Each wall was a different colour—mostly pastel shades. The furniture

19

was a mixture of antique and contemporary and yet it all seemed to mix well, the curtains were soft dull colours, mostly of silk material. It was all harmonious and restful.

In due course Jean produced the inevitable bottle of wine and glasses and as they sat talking and laughing with everyone relaxed, Annette lost some of the feeling of discomfiture she had felt because of Henry Revoir's behaviour. He had been preoccupied with his problems. He had not meant to be rude, she told herself.

Madame Casca sat in the high-backed chair she preferred, her hands folded in her lap, her spotless white collar pristine on her black frock as she smiled at Annette and looked adoringly at her children.

'Why didn't my father let me come out here before?' Annette asked her abruptly.

Madame Casca lifted her glass and with the air of a connoisseur, tasted the wine, nodding approvingly. She looked at Annette and her face was concerned.

'You have not guessed, my child? It is because he loves you. Soon—soon after he was released from the prison camp—' She paused and shuddered. Annette regretted her question for a moment because it had revived sad memories—Monsieur Casca had died in the prison camp.

'After,' Madame Casca went on bravely, 'after he was released and went to England,

20

he learned that he was to become paralysed. It might take years—it could be months. He came here at his friend *le Colonel's* request. *Le Colonel* said, as he said to us all: "We were allies then, we are allies now. What I have is yours." A wonderful man, *le Colonel,'* said Madame Casca proudly. 'We, who lost everything in France, found it again here. So your father was given that little house and Pierre to serve him and we all loved him. We tried to make him laugh and not to lose hope.'

'So he has been ill for many years,' Annette cried. 'But I—I would have loved to come and care for him.' Her voice thickened for a moment.

Madame Casca nodded understandingly 'That I know, but your father loves you, *chérie.* It is many a time that he has said to me: "Of a certainty it would not be fair—she is young. She must lead her own life. I could not have her tied to me. A young lovely girl to nurse a paralysed cripple." That, my child, I have heard him say often. "No," he would tell me, "she must not know," ' Madame Casca finished dramatically.

Annette bent her head to hide the tears in her eyes.

'I wish—' she began, but what was the use of wishing? At least she was here now.

'Why did he send for me now?' she asked instead.

Madame Casca looked thoughtful while

21

Jean refilled the wine glasses, pausing by his mother to touch her lightly on the cheek.

'Confession is good for the soul, *Maman,*' he said lightly. 'Let us hope the little one will not be angry with you.' He smiled at Annette. 'Could you be angry?'

'I could never be angry with your mother,' she said gravely. 'She has been too good to me.' She waited patiently while the Frenchwoman sipped her wine.

At last Madame Casca was ready to talk. 'My child, it was I! You will understand that it took courage, no? Your father, he was sad—very sad. I see that he longs for his child, but is too unselfish to admit it. He battles—his heart with his conscience. I think to myself: now that child, she is no more a child. She is a young woman ripe for marriage. It is only fitting that she should come before she finds herself a husband. She should see her father first, so—' She paused and her eyes were bright as she looked inquiringly at Annette. 'I was right?'

Jean had gone to sit by Annette's side, had taken her hand in his pretending to study it, flexing each finger slowly, saying softly, 'So tiny; the hands of a fairy like rose petals.'

She wished he would not interrupt and she tried to free her hand, but he clung to it, laughing at her, trying to distract her while she wanted to listen to what Madame Casca had to say.

'Of course you were right, Madame,'

Annette said quickly. 'So?'

'So I went to "Himself" and said that it was only right that you should be with your father,' Madame Casca said, and spread out her hands expressively. 'So—I spoke to "Himself" and here you are. *Voila.*'

' "Himself" sent for me?' Annette said, looking bewildered. 'But why—why didn't "Himself" tell my father to send for me? Oh, of course—my father might have refused. I'm most grateful to you, Madame.'

Madame Casca was beaming, her small double chin wobbling, as she said, ' "Himself" has some good points. He makes the instant decision and then acts. The same day the cable was sent to you, the same day he cabled the money for the tickets—everything.'

'So I—we owe "Himself" the money for my fare,' Annette said. Suddenly she could not speak as she watched their faces, and was afraid.

'I have no money. I suppose my father—' She stopped again and her hand flew to her mouth. Her eyes looked very young and frightened as she stared at the Cascas' faces. 'Has my father got enough money?'

'He has no money, my child,' Madame Casca said compassionately and yet as if it was the most natural state in the world. 'We none of us have any money. I told you. We gave all to France.' She beamed. 'Do not let it concern you, my child. Do not forget he has not been

23

able to work.'

'But every month he sent money to the bank for me,' Annette pointed out, her brow furrowed with unpleasant thoughts. She was horribly afraid. Afraid to put her fear into words.

Madame Casca nodded genially. 'That was *le Colonel's* money,' she said gently.

'And when *le Colonel* died?' Annette jumped to her feet, unable to sit still. She leant on the wooden railing, gazing down at the rocks below. 'So I am a pauper,' she said slowly.

She was horrified at the word. What had made it come into her head? Inwardly she writhed. It was Henry Revoir's money. No wonder he looked so supercilious, so—so smug. Her eyes burned with tears of shame. Did he think she knew? Did he think she had calmly, complacently accepted? She swung round, looking at them defiantly. 'I'll pay back every penny. I won't accept charity.'

Jean was by her side now, one arm round her shoulder, hugging her.

'Hush, my angel. No need to be so unhappy. The Seigneur can well afford to keep us all. He has so much money.' He waved an airy hand.

Annette stood stiffly, fighting the tears. 'It isn't that—it's the principle of the thing.'

There was the sound of a knock, of a mascuine voice. Madeleine, with one of her lovely cat-like movements, slid off the couch

24

and hurried away. She returned almost at once with a short plump man who might have stepped out of a cartoon, Annette thought, her mind distracted for a moment as she was introduced to a caricature of a Frenchman, who gesticulated, kissed her hand with a flourish and kept stroking his small black beard.

As he spoke to Madame Casca, Annette thought of what she had just learned. The humiliation of it. Her heart seemed to swell inside her so that she could not breathe as she battled with her distress. She must pay 'Himself' back all she owed him. But how could she? It would take a lifetime.

'Mademoiselle.' The *avocat,* Jacques le Roy, the funny little Frenchman, spoke to her gravely. He had a few questions, if she would be so gracious? Annette sat down feeling limp and near tears. How could she ever pay Henry Revoir back? Thirteen years she had been dependent on the Revoirs. How could she pay them back? She brushed back her hair with a weary hand and answered obediently the many questions the *avocat* asked.

As she spoke almost automatically, her unhappy mind running in circles like a frightened rabbit, unable to forget the overwhelming honor of the knowledge that she and her father had *nothing,* Annette was quite unaware of the fact that she was painting an accurate picture of her unhappy life in

25

England. Nor was she aware, perhaps, quite how unhappy she had been.

'Aunt' Maggie, with whom Annette had lived, had known her father in their youth, and when he had sent his wife and baby back to England, he had been desperate and had thought of Maggie at once. She lived in a remote village, had private means and a flourishing school, he knew. In addition, he remembered, she had a kind heart. But he must have forgotten that Maggie had once hoped he would marry her and so she never quite forgave Annette's mother, and although she was kind to them, let them have a little cottage, she worked Annette's mother hard and had no patience or sympathy with her during the long years when no one knew what had happened to Randal Laleham.

When Mrs. Laleham died and Annette was left alone, Aunt Maggie had been more loving, but by then Annette was older and could read between the lines and remember her 'Aunt's' coldness to the sick mother and her indifference to the child. So although outwardly Annette had seemed happy enough, her heart was always sore and the feeling of a loss that could never be replaced persisted. She had counted so much on her father; when he returned she had been overjoyed. Then he had gone away, off across the world, pleading a job that took him to distant lands Annette and 'Aunt' Maggie had to accept the fact that

26

he did not want them.

Maybe it embittered 'Aunt' Maggie; maybe she was just made that way, but although she was coolly 'kind' to the young girl, she worked her hard and made good use of her. Annette's neat mending and her exquisite sewing was always useful and gradually she learned to substitute for many of the employees at the school. She learned to be housekeeper; cook; to supervise games, and taught French. But, she admitted now, she received no salary. After all, it was her home.

'So your aunt—I mean your aunt by courtesy,' the *avocat* corrected himself. 'She collected your monthly allowance?'

The question caught Annette unawares and she felt her face suddenly hot. 'Yes.'

The *avocat* stared at her. 'What is wrong?' Annette found herself twisting her hands. 'N— nothing.'

'You personally received none of the money?' he persisted.

'Well, I had my clothes and food and—' Annette said.

'You also worked,' he pointed out, his voice dry. 'Yet you received no salary. Why did you not demand?'

Annette blushed again 'I didn't think of it. If I wanted anything, I asked and—and she gave me money.' She bent her head, hiding her eyes from the bright beady inquiring eyes of the *avocat.* That was not quite true. 'Aunt'

Maggie had hated parting with money. It had been a battle royal every time Annette needed new clothes, so she had started to earn extra money by baby-sitting or by embroidering for her friends, all of whom were on her side and never gave her away to her aunt. Once Maggie had found out, then there would have been a row.

Monsieur le Roy thanked her formally, bowed to them all and left them. Jean saw him off the premises. On his return Jean suggested another glass of wine, but Annette tried to refuse. She felt sleepy, finding it hard to think. All she knew was that she felt a little happier, no longer quite so mortified at the thought of owing so much to Henry Revoir.

Perhaps Madame Casca made a secret sign to her children, for they drifted away, leaving Annette alone with the middle-aged Frenchwoman.

'My child,' she said softly as she pulled her chair closer to Annette's and laid her hand on the girl's. 'I can see the shock and the pain in your face, but do not grieve so much. It was because he loved your father that *le Colonel* helped him. When you are rich it is good to help others. It is often hard to accept the gifts. Remember it is easier to give than to receive,' she said, and the compassion in her voice was almost too much for Annette's composure.

'I—d-don't mind *le Colonel* giving us money,' she confessed, her voice husky. 'It—

it's being indebted to—to "Himself" that I find hard to accept—' She caught back a sob.

Madame Casca stared at her in dismay. 'But you do not know him?'

'He came this afternoon. He was—was—' She hesitated and then confessed: 'He treated me like a child. I hated it,' she said violently, and then gave a little apologetic laugh, looking at her companion, expecting to see amusement on her face. But Madame Casca was not amused. She looked shocked.

'But that is unforgivable, *chèrie,* and of a wickedness not to be endured. That he should insult you—a woman!' Her voice was indignant.

Quite suddenly Annette was able to laugh. And to laugh with real humour. What a fuss she was making about nothing. Madame had made her see it as it truly was—just a joke.

'He didn't insult me,' Annette said. 'The thing was I wore my best dress and tried terribly hard to look nice and then—then he just didn't see me at all—' she finished honestly, her voice naive.

Madame patted her hand 'Give him time, my child. He may have had troubles. Henri Revoir is a man who cannot see far because he is so occupied with things that are close. How can I say it?' she asked, moving her hands expressively. 'He worries about the small things and overlooks the large. He sees the petty pinpricks but not the glorious vistas.'

29

She went on as she waved an airy hand towards the ocean. 'See, you see that beauty— yes? I see that beauty. But "Himself"? All he can see is a vast amount of water being wasted. He thinks to himself, how sad. Harnessed, that ocean could produce a great many c.c.'s of electricity. Is it c.c.'s, my child, in electricity? But no matter; to him everything is wasted unless it is used. Ah, *quelle drole.* The poor man How he loses happiness by such a view of life.' She threw up her hands in mock horror.

Annette could not keep herself from laughing. She kissed the Frenchwoman warmly. 'You do me so much good,' she said, her voice affectionate.

'I do?' Madame Casca was surprised. 'But I have done nothing.'

Annette laughed again and left her, surprised to see how long she had stayed, hurrying up the steep, winding lane. She saw a path twisting and turning through the trees. She took it, hoping it was a short cut to the house. How long had her father been alone? The sound of chattering made her look up, and there, staring worriedly down through the green leaves, was the little white face of a monkey. It was so sweet. Annette stopped, holding out her hand invitingly, but of course as she had no biscuit the monkey only chattered shrilly and swung off out of sight. It was cool here in the shadow of the trees, and only the quiet noises of the wildlife to form a background chorus.

The path emerged just below the house, but hearing voices she hesitated, sheltering behind a tall bush of pale pink camellias, not wanting to bump into Henry Revoir.

She had recognized his voice at once, but now it was Jacques le Roy speaking. 'But it is absurd, fantastic,' he was saying. 'Already your life, it has complications enough. There is no need to feel this responsibility for her. She will find a husband. Pretty, sensible, she is a biddable child. She will make a good marriage and you can forget her.'

Annette caught her breath painfully. Were they—could they be talking about her?

'Her father is worried about her future,' Henry Revoir said.

'*Mais certainement,*' the *avocat* replied quickly, 'it is natural for him to worry. But she will be all right. If all else fails, there is always Jean Casca.'

'Jean Casca?' Henry Revoir sounded angry. 'Jean Casca—what has he to offer a girl?' he asked sarcastically.

'He is handsome—amusing,' Jacques pointed out.

'Jean Casca is a wastrel. Heaven help the girl he marries,' was Henry Revoir's comment,

Annette shrunk back under the bush's sheltering branches. So long as they did not see her. Oh, but it was too humiliating to be discussed like this!

'Marriage can make a man,' the *avocat* offered advice.

'And break a woman,' Henry Revoir retorted angrily. 'Let's have no more talk of Jean Casca.'

'But Monsieur should give the matter much thought.' Jacques le Roy sounded more servile. Annette could picture him rubbing his hands together. 'I beg of you not to rush into it.'

Henry Revoir interrupted him, his voice icy. 'I have no intention of rushing into anything. When I require your advice I will ask for it.'

'*Mais naturellement, monsieur,* it is for you to decide. I wish you good day, *monsieur.*' Jacques le Roy now sounded pleased, almost, Annette found herself thinking, as if he had won the battle.

She waited until she heard the sound of a car as it was started and driven away. Now she could look round her, see the small birds flitting by, accepting her as part of the scenery, the butterflies, so fantastic both in size and colour. In the big trees, the Indian mynahs had begun their shrill chattering, a sign that the sun was sinking and the afternoon soon over. When she was sure there was no one left to see her she began to walk towards the small pink house, looking down at the carpet of tiny white flowers that covered the ground. The angry screeching of the green parakeets startled her. She looked up and found herself gazing at

Henry Revoir.

'So we meet again,' he said.

For a moment she was terrified. Did he know the had overheard that conversation? Would he ask her how long she had been there? Could she lie to him?

'Where have you been all the afternoon?' he demanded.

'Visiting the Cascas.' Remembering his unkind remarks about Jean, she wondered how he would react.

'I see,' he merely grunted. 'How old are you?' he asked curtly.

She glared at him. 'Eighteen,' she said crossly.

He was frowning at her. 'I see,' he said. What a firm mouth he had, she thought—what a stubborn chin. All her original awe of him returned, far worse than it had been before. 'You like the Cascas?' he asked.

'Oh yes,' she said very quickly, unconsciously clasping her hands together. 'They have been so kind. Madame Casca makes me laugh, even when I am sad. She can show me where I am wrong, when I exaggerate.' She stopped, startled by her own flow of words.

'You are sad? You said you liked life on the Island,' he reminded her sternly.

She brushed back the fringe on her forehead. 'I am sad about my father,' she admitted. She found the needed courage. 'Is

33

there nothing we can do for him?'

He saw the way her mouth trembled as she fought for control.

'He has seen specialists.' His voice was gentle. 'I promise you that everything that can be done has been. Nothing has been left undone. He a happy man now, so happy to have you with him.'

She clasped her fingers again, twisting them staring at him.

'If only I could do something,' she said desperately.

'Come, let us go inside. Just make him happy,' Henry Revoir told her, taking her arm, guiding her along the path for suddenly her eyes wen full of tears and she could not see. 'Just make him happy, that is all we can do.'

CHAPTER THREE

It was as if time stood still during the next few weeks for Annette. Her love and anxiety for her father drove all other thoughts from her mind so that it no longer seemed so terrible to be under an obligation to 'Himself'; indeed, nothing mattered but her father.

As he grew more frail and his voice became a tired whisper, she felt her heart must surely break. Yet he seemed so happy and his eyes were so bright with love when he saw her that she tried hard to hide her emotion, to act as if everything was normal. Knowing how short their time together must be, she could hardly bear to leave him for a moment, and yet if she did not go out into the sunshine or meet people, it worried him. She acquired the habit of slipping out of the house during Henry Revoir's daily visit.

Her feet shod in rope-soled shoes, wearing jeans and a thin shirt, and of course the inevitable hat and dark glasses, Annette would scramble over the slippery rocks on the sea shore, bending over the tiny pools to gaze in wonder at the waving fronds of the delicate undersea plants, or trying to catch in her hands the small gaily-coloured fish. But then she would start to worry and find herself climbing the hill again. Sometimes she looked in on the Cascas for a quick greeting, though she rarely stayed for more than a few moments, nor did they try to persuade her, so that she knew that they too recognized the urgency of her need to be with her father.

If Henry Revoir was still at the little house, Annette would find somewhere where she would be out of sight and sit listening to the deep rumble of his voice, too far away to make out what he was saying, yet knowing when he was angry or exasperated, or even bewildered, because of the way his voice changed. Afterwards, when Henry had gone, her father would tell her what was troubling the

Seigneur. Randal Laleham could talk happily for hours about the Island, the Revoirs and the Islanders.

'Life is so difficult for Henry,' he would say, holding Annette's hand in his, smiling at her. 'I wonder, can you see that? First he goes to an English school, then comes the war and his mother whisks him off to America and a different kind of education. He hears little about his father and brother; his mother is afraid of Henry's French blood.'

Annette smiled as her father pulled a wry face. 'His mother, poor woman. To be so jealous of a boy's father and of his country! Henry's whole outlook is either British or American; he never thought to be Seigneur, to hold the future of these people in his hand, to be responsible for them. He takes his responsibilities very seriously and realizes the crass stupidity of allowing people to become dependent on you.'

'Why is it stupid?' Annette asked, holding his hand against her cheek. She thought how very different from the way the Cascas saw the situation was her father's view.

Her father eased his aching body carefully as if trying to hide the pain he felt. 'Because it is false kindness,' he said. 'If you are generous and strong, allowing others to lean on you, what happens if you go away? Those you have supported will collapse. People must be taught to stand alone, accepting help only on the understanding that they will repay it.

'No Islander thinks of repaying the Revoirs. They see it as Henry's inherited duty to go on supporting them for ever. They do not see how generous the Revoirs have been. The Islanders take everything for granted; as their right. *Le Colonel,* my dear friend, had a heart of gold, but his head, it was always in the clouds. In a way, I pity Henry's mother. Such a man as *le Colonel* should never marry. Fortunately for Henry's mother, she had a fortune of her own.'

Randal Laleham smiled wryly at his daughter. 'Money we affect to despise, my darling child, but it has its uses. *Le Colonel* saw himself as the father of these people, their saviour—but what he failed to see was that the economics of the world are changing and that even a great fortune subjected to taxes and a constant drain can dwindle away. Henry is not as wealthy as his father was. Suppose the day comes when he can no longer shoulder this burden?'

'But—' Annette ran her hand through her dark curly hair, her eyes were worried, *'could* Henry lose all his money?'

'It is true that it is not probable, but it is possible. That is why he wishes all the Islanders to become shareholders in the Island, to run it on an independent basis, to have a parliament of its own, so that he can seek advice and help, so that they all feel the Island belongs to them,' her father explained.

'They think that now,' Annette pointed out. 'They depend utterly on him.'

'That is what Henry wishes to alter. The trouble is that Henry suffers under a great disadvantage. He was not known here. The Islanders resented his mother's attitude. He is not one of them. I remember how a few years ago Henry visited the Island because he wanted to know his father and his brother. They were all strangers. It was pathetic. Growing up away from them was a terrible mistake. They all tried to like and understand one another, but—' He shrugged sadly, and Pierre chose that moment to bring out two bowls of iced *bouillon,* his dark face anxious as he stared at his master and then looked at Annette.

She smiled back reassuringly and took the bowls. *'Merci,* Pierre.' What would they do without dear faithful slow-thinking Pierre, whose huge muscled arms lifted her father so easily, whose great scarred hands were as tender as any mother's?

'Poor Henry,' she said thoughtfully as she put a cushion behind her father's back and arranged the small table by his side for the bowl of soup. 'It must have been a shock to find he had inherited the Island.'

'It certainly was—his whole life was changed. He had an excellent post in London,' her father told her as he dutifully sipped the *bouillon.* 'He had a central flat, his own group of friends. In fact, a pleasant and satisfactory life. An efficiency expert, he enjoyed his work and had an extremely promising future. Naturally he always thought that Maurice, his brother, would be the next Seigneur. No one, least of all Henry, expected his brother and father would die within a few days of one another.'

Annette had finished and laid down the bowl. What heavy weather her poor father was making of the delicious liquid. Should she suggest he need not drink it—or would that show that she had noticed his difficulty?

'I gather that as soon as he arrived here, things began to go wrong,' she said slowly, clasping her hands round her knees, trying to hide the anxiousness she was afraid must show in her eyes.

'I'm afraid so. They don't like his hair—his accent—his rather pedantic scholarly French. He did not have a chance. I have tried to advise him. Patience and understanding can solve the problem and I know Henry will do his best, but the Islanders seemed determined to irritate and frustrate him,' her father told her.

'Is all the Island Henry's?' she asked.

'Originally it all belonged to the Revoirs, but *le Colonel* sold some of it to those of his countrymen he trusted. He saw the Island as a country in miniature with everyone working for the common good. But he did not see how things would develop, that he would be used. The Islanders are so accustomed to his help and generosity that they know no other life, nor do they wish to know of another way of living. This is so simple.'

He gave her the empty bowl and wiped his mouth on the small embroidered napkin. 'Like the rest of the Islanders, after the war I was offered a home by my friend Henri Revoir, a house, a pension, affection. The Islanders see this as their right. Neither I nor Henry can understand why they cannot see that the war ended over fifteen years ago. There has been time to gather up the pieces; in any case, the younger generation have no excuse. Take Jean Casca—nice enough, charming—but bone lazy and selfish.'

Annette was surprised by the suddenly stern note in her father's voice. 'You may find this difficult to believe, but he is a qualified accountant. *Le Colonel* paid for his education and training, yet Jean prefers to live on his mother's pension and to play at painting. He has no sense of responsibility—no desire to repay any of the generosity he has enjoyed. Henry asked his assistance once when he was struggling with some new and intricate tax assessment for the Island—and do you know what Jean said?' Randal's voice was harsh for a moment. 'He told Henry that he was not a clerk!'

'Oh no,' Annette whispered. 'Has Jean no

pride? They say they despise Henry,' she went on, 'because he is not a Frenchman, but how can you take from someone you despise?'

'Pride?' Her father patted her hand gently. 'My dear, those of us who can afford pride rarely have it. It is the ones who are truly dependent who find it sometimes hard.' His voice was sad. 'You know that I have nothing, my darling child?' His eyes searched her face anxiously. 'I am sad that I have nothing to leave you.'

She caught his hand and kissed it, her eyes full of tears.

'Don't, don't,' she said unhappily. 'You were so ill. You lost everything. Madame Casca told me. Had you been well, you would never have accepted charity.'

She wondered why he closed his eyes for a moment. When he spoke again he sounded desperately tired. 'When it is given with love, my darling, it is never charity. That is a cold word, a cruel, ugly word. Remember always that it is difficult to receive gracefully, yet sometimes we have no alternative. Then—then we must try to repay the gift in some other way, not necessarily with money. It could be with affection, kindness.'

It seemed to require a great effort on his part, she noticed worriedly, but he withdrew a gold hunter watch from his pocket. He put it in her hand, holding both her hands over it with his.

'My darling, this I am giving to you. On it is a small key. That key will unlock a tin box you will find in my cupboard. Inside it are all the notes I have collected about the Revoirs. Always I planned to write a book about them, but I have left it too late.'

'Daddy, don't,' she cried out, putting her face on his hands, closing her eyes. 'Don't talk like that, please.'

His smile was tender. 'Remember that my last weeks have been very happy ones. Remember I am very tired and that sometimes the pain is very hard to bear. Remember that I love you, that I will always be near you. One day when you are older and have more patience, read the notes I have written about the Revoirs. It seems to me that what is written there could save the Island and its people.' He leaned back, his face white and drawn, the cheek bones standing out like gaunt mountains.

'I will read it. I will,' began Annette, then heard the welcome sound of a car.

Scrambling to her feet, she patted her rumpled hair, looked in the mirror at the flushed cheeks, the tear-filled eyes. And Henry Revoir walked in, apologetically saying:

'I forgot to ask you about the Nerfuti Mills, sir. Are you too tired?'

Randal Laleham smiled. Annette thought for one heartbreaking moment that he looked relieved. She was ashamed of her own

42

emotional state, but it was not so easy to hide her unhappiness.

'I am never too tired to help you, my boy,' Randal said gently.

Henry drew up a chair and unfolded an important looking document. 'I don't know what I'd do without you, sir.' He glanced at Annette and she saw momentary disapproval in his eyes.

She hurried to her bedroom, there to have a good cry, and then she bathed her eyes in cold water, carefully making up her face afterwards. She would not be so weak again. She could hear her father laughing. How good Henry was to him. Henry had many good points, despite what the Cascas and the Islanders thought.

She went back to the veranda and asked if the two men would like coffee. In the kitchen, as she helped Pierre prepare the tray, she listened to Henry's deep voice. She tried not to think of the future when she would be alone again, not to worry about what she would do, or to remember the debt she already owed the Revoirs.

It was quite a gay little party on the veranda. Her father played cribbage, a game they both enjoyed. It was quite late for them when she kissed him good night and went to her bedroom.

It was Pierre's animal-like moan that awoke her. She could see from the doorway of the room that already her father had left them. He looked so relaxed, a small smile on his mouth.

'Pierre, don't,' Annette said, instinctively trying to comfort the old Creole, who stood with the tears running down his dark cheeks. 'Don't.' Then she turned away, burying her face in her hands, realising the truth.

All too soon there were people there to intrude on her grief, yet with the best of intentions. Madame Casca putting on coffee, murmuring comforting words; Henry Revoir himself, staring down at her strangely, for she had no idea how extremely young and frightened she looked, with her pinched mouth, her eyes welling with the tears she struggled to control.

It seemed the most natural thing in the world for Henry to take her in his arms, to hold her close to his heart, to tell her to cry, not to fight it.

Annette, as the sobs shook her body and the tears poured down her cheeks, thought of all the wasted years—years she might have spent with her father, loving him, nursing him; years he had denied her because he loved her so much. She was vaguely aware that Henry was holding her close, that his voice was kind. All she realized was that never had she felt so safe, so comforted, and as she managed to stop crying at last, and looked up apologetically into his face, she saw that there

44

was no need for words. Henry understood; and understanding, forgave her for her weakness in breaking down.

CHAPTER FOUR

It was all like a nightmare, with people's faces floating in and out of her vision, their compassionate voices, Pierre's perpetual tears and, above all, the utter desolation. Tossing and turning in the huge feather bed in the Cascas' house, Annette wondered how she could bear it. There were no words of comfort, not even from Henry now, for since he had directed Madame Casca to look after Annette, he had stayed noticeably away.

Even the Cascas had remarked on it, and something of the picture that Annette's father had built up in her mind of a Henry more sinned against than sinning, battling against overwhelming odds, doing his very best, began to fade, become distorted. Now in the affectionate circle of the Cascas, Annette heard tales of Henry's coldness, his lack of thought, his 'modern' ways. And then she began to think how much all these people owed the Revoirs—and that brought her unhappy thoughts to the question of herself.

What was she going to do? How could she ask Henry for more money? Yet ask she must.

There were no jobs on the Island, Madame had said sadly, but, she had added, Annette need not worry, for she would inherit her father's pension—and the Frenchwoman had smiled as if that settled everything. Of course it did not. No girl with an ounce of pride in her could accept charity—for this would be charity; it would be given without love.

Not even sleeping pills could help her sleep as during the two nights before the funeral she battled with her problem through the long frightening hours before the dawn. If Henry Revoir would lend her the money for her fare back to England, perhaps she could get a job there. Even if it took her years, she would repay him. That she could promise him.

It was a perfect day as they went to the lovely flower-filled cemetery on the mountain high up above the small villages Annette was amazed at the crowd that had gathered, at the great armfuls of sweet-smelling flowers, at the sympathetic faces of every colour and age. Her hand soon ached from the compassionate handshakes, her face felt stiff with the effort not to cry as in turn these people came to tell her how much they had admired and loved her father.

She stood by Henry Revoir's side, a slight girl in a black frock, borrowed from Madeleine and hastily altered by Madame Casca—and a small black hat from the latter's wardrobe. Henry kept glancing down at her anxiously.

46

The sun streamed down mercilessly and for once there was no breeze to relieve the heat. The scent of the flowers was sickly and almost overpowering.

The beautiful service read by the husky-voiced priest was nearly Annette's undoing, and it was with relief that she found herself after the final ceremonies alone with Henry Revoir for a moment.

'I shall miss him,' Henry said soberly. He looked at the exhausted young face and hesitated for a moment.

'Annette,' he said slowly, addressing her for the first time by her Christian name, she realized. She looked up at him with full eyes. If only she could be alone! 'It is my wish,' he went on, his voice stiff and formal because of his nervousness, 'my wish that you stay at the Chateau while we discuss your future.'

Her eyes widened with fear, horror and shame. 'I have made arrangements for you to be chaperoned by Madame Lascie, one of my oldest friends. I think you met her just now,' Henry went on. 'There she is, see, by the jacaranda tree. That little old lady with the black cape and feathered hat. See her?' He waited for Annette to nod, but she was not understanding a word of what he was saying. She was battling with a terrible fear.

'Madame Casca,' she whispered. Why couldn't he leave her alone? Just let her go back to the little pink house, to Pierre.

'She has gone away.' He took a deep breath. 'I spoke to her on the subject and she agreed it would be more seemly if you lived at the Chateau.'

'Seemly?' Annette said, almost stupidly. Why did he look so ill at ease? What did he want to talk to her about? The money she already owed him? Oh, it was too much! She half turned away, hoping he had not seen her tears. 'Can't I go home?' she asked, like a child.

'You cannot stay in the *campement* alone,' he said curtly. 'I have it all arranged. Already your clothes are at the Chateau. Come, we will go now,' he finished sternly, and turned away.

She followed him resentfully. Now the crowds of people in their heavy black mourning were drifting away, but many smiled at her or waved a hand. There were so many faces she had never seen before, yet they all looked at her as if she was a friend, and it comforted her. If only she could find some work to do on the Island, she thought desperately, for she did not want to leave it.

Henry settled her in the cream car and then took the wheel. As if able to read her thoughts, he said, 'Madame Lascie has her own car and her own chauffeur. You need not see much of her. She is very old and easily tired. She will have her own apartment at the Chateau.'

It took some time to weave their way through the crowds on the main road, the

48

many walkers, the few big cars, several pony traps. But at last they were free and he could drive swiftly down the winding, twisting road that clung to the side of the mountain. Although the car was open, Annette could feel little breeze as they travelled, and the lower they got, the hotter the day became. She pulled off her hat and let the air ruffle her hair She sat stiffly, staring ahead of her, knowing Henry Revoir meant it for the best, but wishing he would let her go to her father's house, there to grieve alone. Only of course it was not her father's house. Everything belonged to Henry. She closed her eyes. How could she ask him to help her still more? Already he must despise her.

Henry slowed up as he turned off the main road. Ahead of them were wide open wrought-iron gates, but a young Creole girl in a voile frock came out of a small squat house and gave them a pert little curtsy.

Annette smiled at her and then looked ahead, her grief momentarily forgotten as she gasped aloud in sheer delight. The drive curved and circled round a vast, close-shaven lawn edged by tall, waving coco-palms. They then reached the Chateau itself. Annette had heard about it; now she stared up at its tall pillars, the long balcony that ran round the house, the carved cherubs all over the tall windows, the tall stone chimneys.

'As an example of architecture,' Henry

Revoir said sarcastically, 'it is not very good, but—'

'I think it's lovely,' Annette said. She loved everything about it, the faded pink colour, the sparkling windows that stood open; the feeling of age, comfort and gracious living.

As the car stopped she gazed round her. The garden was full of flowers and was tidy, yet it had a forlorn air. They were on an escarpment high above a lagoon and she stared in delight at the smooth blue water, the blindingly white sands, the ring of coral rocks and outside the huge rollers racing in to break futilely against the rocks. Henry opened the car door for her and helped her out.

She gazed up at the building. 'It—it looks a happy house,' she said, not sure why she had said it nor what had made her think it.

His tanned face looked glum. 'Think so? It's old, dilapidated and needs too much money spent on it. In other words, it's a white elephant.'

She showed her dismay plainly. 'Don't you like it?'

He coloured a little, looking right down into her amazed eyes.

'It isn't a question of like or dislike,' he told her crossly. 'It's a question of whether the money that ought to be spent on it wouldn't be better spent elsewhere.' He put his hand under her elbow as they climbed the four shallow steps that led to the colonnade. 'I hate waste,' he said almost savagely.

The huge wooden front door swung open majestically and a tall, fat Creole stood there, immaculately clad in a white suit, and wearing spotless white gloves. He held the door back and bowed formally.

'This is Rennie,' Henry said gravely, but there was a twinkle in his eye.

Annette glanced at the tall Creole and smiled. He frowned a little and then his dark face was creased into a friendly smile as he bowed again.

In the hall she glanced around curiously. It was an enormous hall, lofty with a gallery running round it and two staircases going up to the gallery, joined together on the ground and dividing halfway up like branches of a tree. There were four huge chandeliers swinging from the distant ceiling. On the walls were huge oil paintings; one was a seascape; another—

'You will like to go to your room and rest,' Henry said quietly. 'This is Cecile—your own maid.'

Annette smiled at the young girl, who curtsied. She wore a pale pink frock with a tiny pleated white apron over it. Annette noticed that both the frock and apron were clean but torn.

Henry said curtly, 'Annette, your father would have hated you to wear black; you know how he loathed it. I suggest you bath, have a

51

sleep, put on something bright and then come down to my study. We have to talk.' He walked with her to the foot of the stairs and hesitated. 'You like the Chateau?' He sounded surprised.

'I love it,' Annette told him quickly. 'It has so much character—if these walls could talk—' Through an open door in the hall she had caught a glimpse of a beautiful room, its walls hung with a gold and white silk; there was a thick white carpet, huge chairs covered with gold and white brocade, vases of stiffly-arranged flowers.

'It needs a mistress,' he said, turning away. 'It is many years since a woman reigned here.'

She watched him walk down the hall slowly. His broad shoulders seemed to droop a little as if he was tired, or depressed. What a fine man he was, and yet so difficult. She did wish so much that she had not to ask him for a favour. Even though it was a loan only, would he believe that? Embittered by the Islanders' selfish acceptance of his generosity, might he not imagine she was the same?

She walked up the wide stairs slowly, hearing the crisp rustle of the Creole girl's starched frock behind her. At the top, Cecile gave a little bob and led the way down past closed doors until she flung one wide open and stood back.

Annette stood in the doorway and stared, her eyes widening. It was not a very big room, but the bed was a beautiful antique, soft white curtains hanging down from a small crown attached to the wall above it. There was an old-fashioned wash-stand with a rose and white china jug and bowl, a massive wardrobe, a balcony with the french windows wide open. She went to stand there, to stare out at the garden, at the smooth lagoon, the feathery casuarina trees. Birds were singing, but she could not see them. She was suddenly aware that little Cecile was staring at her, one dark finger in her mouth.

'I would like a bath, Cecile,' Annette said.

The young girl beamed. 'But of course, *messie,*' she said, and almost ran down the corridor, flinging open another door, and vanished into the room. Annette followed more sedately and then had to fight back the laughter as she saw the great bathtub in the enormous room. Cecile was turning on the tap and a cloud of steam came pouring out and then brownish hot water. The girl straightened and beamed, giving an expressive wave of her hands and looking as proud as if she had performed some miracle.

'I will get the towels,' she said, and scurried down the corridor again.

Annette felt infinitely better for the bath, and after fifteen minutes of lying on the soft feather bed gazing up at the spotless white curtains and noting the tiny holes, she dressed with more confidence than she had hoped to have. She chose a soft cream silk frock. She had made it herself out of an Indian sari that Jean had bought for her in the market. Her father had been amazed at her skill with her needle. 'Another of your many admirable French traits,' he had said. Her father.

Annette closed her eyes quickly, fighting the tears. She must not grieve. She had read somewhere that if you grieve you hinder the progress of the one you have lost; that grief holds him back, keeps him earthbound. But it was terribly hard not to grieve all the same.

She found her confidence oozing away as she walked down the wide staircase to the hall. What did Henry want to talk to her about? Had her father made him feel responsible for her future?

Rennie appeared from nowhere and walked to meet her and then led her to a door. He knocked twice, sharply, gave her a little bow and retired. She stared after the huge figure and thought that here was another good servant, another such as Pierre.

The door was jerked open and there was Henry, glowering at her. Her already frightened heart seemed to turn a somersault, making her catch her breath, causing her eyes to grow big and scared.

'I—I hope I wasn't too long,' she said nervously as she entered the room.

He pulled out a stiff upright chair with huge carved arms and she sat down obediently. And then found that the chair was either too big

54

or her legs too short, for there were her feet dangling like a child's. It did not add to her confidence, and when she saw him looking at her and imagined a smile twisted his mouth, it increased her nervousness so that she began to stutter.

'I know you've d-done everything for my f-father and—and I'm t-terribly grateful.' She paused and took a deep breath, twisting her fingers together unconsciously, two bright flags of colour in her cheeks. 'I—I wondered if you would be so g-good as to lend me m-my fare to England and I'll get a job and—and.

Had he got to stare at her like that? She moved uneasily in the chair and wished he would speak. The silence seemed to last for ever until, in despair, she broke it again.

'I know you despise people who take everything, and I agree, b-but sometimes it's difficult—and I will pay you back,' she said, and suddenly desperation gave her courage and she lifted her head, tilting her small chin, her eyes brave. 'I wish my father need not have been dependent.'

'There was no question of dependence,' Henry said coldly. 'He was my father's friend. Had the positions been reversed, he would have looked after my father. There is no need to be dramatic.'

Her cheeks burned under the rebuke. 'I didn't mean—'

Obviously he was not listening. He leant

55

back in his chair, his arms folded. He looked like a judge—cold, severe, utterly just—and horribly alarming. Was this the same man who had held her close to his heart? Who had comforted her, had shown a wonderful understanding and compassion?

'You talk of paying me back,' Henry said. 'You require another loan?' He sounded very businesslike. Then he leaned forward, his eyes narrowed. 'What sort of work do you propose to do in England? Have you been trained for anything?'

Her cheeks still burned as she admitted that she had received no training. 'I worked in my aunt's school. I can type—with two fingers,' she admitted with an honesty he found endearing. Then her voice lifted proudly. 'One thing, I am good at spelling.'

He began to walk about the room, hands clasped behind his back as if he was trying to find the right words. Annette watched him nervously as she tied the corner of her hankie into a series of knots. What an extraordinarily handsome man he was. If only he did not get cross so quickly, or look so horribly stern. Maybe it was just his manner, for he could be very kind. The difficulty was to know what you had said or done to annoy him.

She looked round the room curiously. The walls were panelled with a dark wood; the desk was huge, made of black wood with great curved carved legs. Over the windows were growing massed leaves of a dark green creeper. It was a depressing room, dark, awesome.

When he stopped before her she jumped and hoped he had not noticed. His voice rasped as if with annoyance and exasperation. 'You are serious about wanting to repay me? Or, I should say, to repay the Revoir family?' he said harshly.

She stared at him, feeling icy cold. How could she ever earn enough money? It would take a lifetime. Her hand flew to her throat nervously.

'Yes. Of c-course,' she said.

'Then—' He stared at her and she felt as if he was waiting to pounce on her. Instinctively she shrank back in the chair, her hands clutching the arms. 'Then will you be my wife?' he said, his voice suddenly quiet.

The room seemed filled with silence, a heavy, frightening silence that seemed to press against her. For a moment she could not speak as she stared up into his face, and then she understood.

He loved her.

The wonder of it filled her with such joy, such breathless happiness that for a moment she could not speak. Now she understood everything—his apparent curtness, his harsh voice. He had been nervous, afraid to tell her.

She seemed to melt with sheer love for him, this wonderful man, this man her father had trusted and whom she had loved from that very first day, although this was the first time she had admitted it. She opened her mouth to tell him, but he spoke first.

Henry had been watching her and now began to walk round the room again, not looking at those wide frightened eyes, the trembling mouth.

'You have enough French blood in you,' he began, 'to accept the fact that it has always been the custom of the French to favour an arranged marriage, or in other words, a marriage of convenience.' He clipped his words curtly. 'I think this would prove an excellent solution to our mutual problem.'

He looked at Annette and saw that she was white as a sheet, her eyes were tightly closed and her small even teeth were biting into her lower lip. 'It will enable me to keep my promise to your father to look after you for the rest of your life,' he went on, his voice impersonal, going to stand by the window, gazing out. 'It will help me very much to have you as my wife.' He raised his voice, wondering if she was listening. 'You speak French fluently. The Islanders have taken you to their hearts. In the short time you have been here you have become one of them, something I doubt if I will ever succeed in doing.' He could not help the bitter disappointment from showing in his voice. He walked round the room again, absentmindedly moving an ashtray. He went on: 'Your father was part of

the legend, you are automatically included.'
He paused for a moment, gazing out of the
window at the smooth lagoon.

He turned to look at her directly, then
moved towards her and saw how she shrank
back in her chair, her eyes like a frightened
animal's

'I won't eat you,' he said crossly.

Faint colour tinged the pale cheeks. 'I—I
know,' she whispered. Her throat was taut with
controlled emotion. The tears pressed against
her eyelids. How stupid she had been. How
could she have been so foolish? How he would
laugh if he knew. Whatever happened, he must
never know.

She looked down at her hands, determined
he should not see the unhappiness in her eyes.
'It's very good of you,' she said slowly.

'Good, nothing,' Henry said, going to sit
down, folding his arms again and scowling at
her.

Her mouth was dry with fear as she sought
for the right words. She looked at him timidly.
If only she did not love him so much. She let
her eyes roam caressingly over his face: that
straight nose, the angry impatient eyes, the
stern, stubborn chin, the dear little mole. She
caught her breath, lowering her head again,
for the tears were so near.

'I—I don't know what to say,' she said
helplessly.

'Then say yes,' he suggested, and smiled for

the first time that day.

Annette tried to smile too, but the effort failed dismally. She began to twist her hands again 'It's so natural for a Frenchman to think on such lines,' she said very slowly. 'But you are English.' Her eyes searched his face anxiously. 'Are you sure you won't regret it? An Englishman marries for love. Surely there is some girl—?' Her voice faltered.

They stared at one another. Honest herself, he thought that she deserved honesty from him.

'There was a girl,' he admitted. 'But we don't see eye to eye about the fundamental and important things of life.' His voice grated for a moment as if he was remembering. 'She is very modern, has no time for sentiment or for the past. She considers the Island is run like a comic opera—that it's a farce—and that I should sell it.'

'Could you?' Annette said softly, her eyes enormous.

He shrugged. 'I was offered an excellent price. It might be better in the long run for the Islanders. They would have to work then—or starve.' His long fingers began to tap impatiently on the desk. 'There are minerals on this island, if we could find them. It costs money to exploit such things, however, and money—' He paused and frowned. 'That's by the way,' he said curtly. 'Let us say only that I'm under no illusions about the girl in question. I would never marry her. I know we could never be happy together.'

Annette leaned forward nervously. No wonder he had never seen her, when his heart already belonged to another. His curtness had not fooled her; she was sure he still loved that girl and had been bitterly hurt by her attitude.

'But could *we* be happy?' she asked him. 'An arranged marriage can only be a success if based on similar backgrounds, shared interests, some affection—' Again her voice faltered. Affection sounded odd to her. She felt far more than affection for him, but he must never guess it.

He was frowning at her. 'But I am fond of you,' he said as if she had suggested the opposite.

She smiled at that, a surprisingly wise smile. 'But you see me as a child,' she told him wistfully.

'Well, you are a child, aren't you?' he said heavily. He began to spin the ashtray on his desk, avoiding her eyes as if trying to find the right words. 'It would be silly to treat you like an *old* woman.' He looked at her for a quick second. 'You will grow up, don't forget. You will be a lovely woman one day.' He spun the ashtray violently. 'I need a wife who will share my life, be attractive, poised. I must interest financiers in projects on the Island; we shall travel—entertain We are bound to have shared interests.' His voice was suddenly very young: 'I promise you, Annette, that I'll do my very best to make you happy.'

She stared at him, her eyes full of tears. Oh, but it was tempting to accept his offer. Suppose she trusted to time and patience on her part to make him love her one day? How wonderful it would be to become his wife; to love and to cherish him. She closed her eyes quickly. She would fight for him, would teach the Islanders to know him for the fine man he was; she would help him to teach them to be independent.

Yet still she hesitated.

'May I think it over?' she asked in a small frightened voice.

Henry nodded. 'Of course you can think it over,' he said curtly, and stood up.

She thanked him meekly and stood up also, following him to the door, hearing him tell her that dinner would be at eight-thirty, and perhaps she should call on Madame Lascie. 'Rennie will take you to her,' Henry said as he closed the door.

Annette stood alone in the vast hall, trembling a little, tempted to run back into the room, to accept his offer there and then. Supposing he changed his mind? Yet what if she was taking too great a risk? Shouldn't she think the matter over?

What could be more agonizing than to be married to a man you love—but who does not love you?

CHAPTER FIVE

Annette's heart had already made the decision in the first moment, but her native French caution advised thought and her English background pointed out that everything was against her. She was afraid of the years that lay ahead, the pain she might cause herself. She loved Henry Revoir, but he was merely marrying her for a reason, for several reasons perhaps. That is, if she accepted him. How could she bear to refuse him? And yet—

As the days passed, she lost some of her awe for Henry. You cannot sit opposite a man for three meals a day without getting to know him a little. He was always very pleasant and polite, extremely courteous to Madame Lascie, the elderly woman who smiled benevolently at Annette and whom Annette soon came to love.

Madame Lascie had but one topic of conversation—the Revoirs, and how wonderful they were. She had a wealthy stock of legends and old stories about the family which Annette never grew tired of hearing. Sometimes Henry talked directly to Annette about the Island, the need for rain, his anxiety because several of the sugar mills had fallen into disrepair, his desire to organize the market, perhaps even control the prices in the different small stores that abounded on the Island. It was adult talk, Annette felt, and it was talk she enjoyed, even, as the days passed, venturing to give an opinion of her own, feeling absurdly proud when he considered it gravely.

It was when she was alone with him that it was so terrible. When Madame Lascie had slowly and painfully mounted the stairs with Rennie's assistance to take her siesta Annette felt the old nervousness taking possession of her. They would sit silently, Annette racking her brains for something to say and then usually saying something so stupid and childish that she was not surprised, though humiliated, to see Henry so often hide an amused smile. It was so much easier wher Madame Lascie was with them, but she could not be with them always, could she? Certainly not when they were married.

Sometimes Annette longed for Henry to demand a decision. She was never sure if she was grateful or resentful because he did not urge her. She was like a child, like the child Henry thought her to be—illogical, inconsistent. If only Henry loved her—if only he would take her in his arms and kiss her. But why waste time in stupid dreams. Henry had made it very plain that he had affection for her, that was all. That he saw her as someone who would make a useful wife, one who would be 'secure', and so he could get rid of his obligation to look after her, as he had promised her father. Was that reason enough for her to risk marrying him?

She took her problem to the little church and knelt inside the bright interior, looking at the beautiful paintings, the fragrant flowers. A great peace enfolded her and as she prayed for wisdom, it seemed to her that her father was very near.

'Dear God, I love him so much. Could I make him happy or will my pain because he does not love me make me become bitter? Might I even change and become hostile like the Islanders—resenting him, hating him?'

She left the church, her decision still not taken, walking past the bright golden and red flowers in the gardens, not seeing the gay little birds with their flashing scarlet backs and long beaks as they swooped into the flowers for honey. She did not even hear the screech of the parakeets as she disturbed their peace as she walked down the hill. Perhaps Madame Casca had returned.

She was at home. The door was ajar and the sound of Madame's shrill excited voice could be heard plainly. Annette knocked several times, afraid to walk in, wondering what was agitating Madame so much. Then the plump little Frenchwoman came hurrying on her stilt-like heels, her cheeks flushed, her arms flung wide open.

'Ah—this delights me. I have but this moment made a return, and here you have

65

come to welcome me,' she said as she kissed Annette on both cheeks. 'And how goes it, *ma petite?*'

In the parlour Annette was given a cup of Madame's delicious coffee and wondered why their conversation was so strained. Was Madame afraid to mention Randal Laleham lest it upset his daughter? She caught Madame Casca watching her worriedly, and it was as if she had given the Frenchwoman a cue.

'You are happy, my child?' she asked softly. 'Happy as it is possible for you to be under the circumstances—or why is it that on your face I see so much—so much trouble?'

'I don't know what to do,' Annette said simply. 'The Seigneur has asked me to marry him.'

There were several conflicting expressions on Madame Casca's face; she looked as if about to speak and then changed her mind. Slowly she put her cup down on the saucer with a little noise and then she asked softly:

'Your decision—without doubt it was—?'

'I haven't given it yet,' Annette admitted. She brushed back her fringe. The shades were drawn against the sun, but the little room seemed stifling. 'I don't know what to say.'

Madame Casca clasped her hands. She looked everywhere in the room as if seeking guidance, then at Annette. 'But of a certainty.' Her dark eyes were worried. 'It is your life, my child. I thought—' She hesitated. 'I thought

66

you had an affection for "Himself".'

Annette's cheeks were afire as she lowered her eyes, trying to hide her secret, and knowing that Madame Casca's shrewd eyes could not fail to recognize the truth. 'I have an affection,' she said slowly. 'That's why I'm troubled. He—he made it sound like a business deal.' In shame she lowered her head, pretending to play with her lace-edged handkerchief, feeling the foolish tears in her eyes.

'Marriages sometimes begin that way,' Madame said in a compassionate voice.

Annette looked up eagerly. 'That's what he said.' She repeated the conversation she had had with Henry. 'Do you really think I could be of assistance to him?' She clasped her hands as she spoke.

'But of course.' Madame Casca sounded surprised at the question. *'Naturellement.* We all loved your father. Now we all love you. You are part of the legend. Far more part of it than "Himself" will ever be,' she said, and added bitterly, 'He wishes to destroy, to pull down all that his father built. It is possible that you can help him to see us with different eyes. It may make all the difference to our survival. But,' Madame's eyes were bright and shrewd as she looked at the young girl's vulnerable face, 'but let us speak for a while of yourself, my child. You are more English than French in your heart—is it of a possibility that you could be happy in a marriage of convenience?'

67

Annette was twisting her fingers together, fidgeting a little. She looked round the familiar room and for a moment it looked alien. She was frightened, but of what, she did not know.

'I don't know,' Annette admitted honestly.

'It is your happiness that is important,' Madame Casca said. 'Forget the Island, and us who have lived on it for so long and so happily until—' She paused, her voice changing again. 'Your father would wish that you follow your heart, my child, for only that way can you find happiness.'

Annette was thinking. Her father had told her to choose a kind man as a husband. Henry was kind. He was wonderful if you were in trouble.

She felt as if the walls of the room were pressing in to smother her. She looked up and surprised a strange smile on Madame Casca's face. Was it an evil smile? It must have been imagination, Annette thought, for the smile instantly vanished and Madame was her old affectionate self.

'It is your life, my child. You do well to consider carefully. If you refuse the Seigneur's offer, have you thought of what else you can do?' she asked anxiously.

Annette stood up, feeling she could not breathe. 'I don't know,' she said wildly. 'I must think.'

Madame walked with her to the veranda, her hand warm on Annette's arm. 'There is no haste, my child. You can take all the time you want.'

But could she? Annette wondered, the blinding sunlight making her blink, fumble in her handbag for her dark glasses. Could she take all the time she liked? You could not expect Henry to wait indefinitely. He needed a wife. That meant—

'But this is a miracle.' Jean Casca's gay voice interrupted her thoughts as he vaulted over the garden gate and came towards her, his lean, handsome face bright. 'I think of you and—lo! Here you are.' Jean seized her hands, turned them over, lifted them to his mouth and deposited a lingering kiss on the palm of each.

Laughing, she withdrew her hands. Jean was impossible at times, and yet such fun!

'I will walk with you to the Chateau,' he announced. 'I have much to tell you, *maman*, but it must wait.'

'*Naturellement*,' his mother said ruefully, and smiled at Annette.

Jean carried the pink fringed sunshade and held it over Annette's head as they strolled slowly up the hill. It was so hot, there was a menacing feeling in the air that was new to Annette, as if something horrible was going to happen. When they reached her father's little house they went into the garden without speaking, almost as if moved by some force stronger than themselves.

Jean perched on the low wall, lighting a cigarette and watching Annette as she wandered disconsolately through the empty rooms, noticed the furniture had been removed. The walls had been scraped, so obviously it was to be repainted, and some new tenant would take possession. She hated the thought. She stood quietly in her father's room, saying softly, feeling he was near her, 'I have those papers, and one day I will make them into a book as you wished.' As she stood there, she also made her decision.

Jean stood up when she joined him. He looked startled.

'But it is unbelievable.' He came to meet her as he spoke and took her hands in his, gazing down at her, his face bewildered. 'A few moments—but a few moments ago, and you were so *distraite,* so sad—and now you are happy. Am I not correct?' His bright eyes flashed.

She had to tilt back her head to look at him. 'I am going to marry the Seigneur,' she told him. 'I have just made the decision.'

She could not understand why he looked so strange. It reminded her of his mother's strange expression. Jean had looked for a moment almost triumphant and then very sad as he lifted her hands to his mouth. He kissed them gently and his voice was tragic. 'But, Annette—have you not known? Did you not see? I wear my heart on my—elbow, as you

70

say in England. It is me you should marry. Me, Jean Casca, who should be your husband.'

It was always hard to know when Jean was playing the fool. Annette decided he was and began to laugh.

Jean was hurt. He dropped her hands at once. 'Ah, you mock me and—' He stroked his small moustache with an unconsciously melodramatic gesture. 'But it is the truth, Annette. I am your slave. I—'

'Jean, it's sweet of you, but—' She looked at her wrist-watch. 'Oh dear, Jean, I do appreciate the honour and—and all that, but I really must go. I had no idea it was so late.'

'You still do not believe me,' he said angrily. 'I do love you,' he almost shouted, and the green parakeets chose that moment to flash down from their favourite casuarina tree and dart over the garden screeching derisively. 'You see,' Jean said, 'not even those—those birds take me seriously.'

Annette struggled with laughter and controlled it. She managed to say mildly, 'But, Jean, would you like to be married? It costs money. What would we live on?' As she spoke she began to walk down the garden path and Jean obediently followed, adjusting the sunshade over her.

'Ah! How hard are the English,' he said, his tragedy forgotten and his eyes twinkling. 'We would live on love, *naturellement.* But if you are serious then I have this to say: I have

71

been to Madagascar to show my paintings and several have been liked.'

'How lovely, Jean,' she said warmly, pausing to smile at him. 'You sold them?'

'Of course I did not sell them,' Jean said, sounding shocked. 'I did not try to sell them. It was enough that the critics approved.'

'But—' Annette began, and stopped, for she was afraid, if she said too much, Jean might think she was considering his offer of marriage seriously. She began to talk again, wishing the hill was not so steep, the sun not so hot. The heat from the road seemed to burn through the thin soles of her shoes, her head was beginning to throb, she longed to be back at the Chateau.

Jean said thoughtfully, after a long silence as they entered a shady patch of road, the trees making a green canopy overhead while the roar of the sea never ceased for a second, 'You forget that you will have a pension. You are your father's daughter.' He said it casually, but she knew he had thought of it before. Instantly she was so angry that she had to battle with her feelings. How right her father had been! All the Islanders were the same, even Jean Casca. They not only took the Revoirs' generosity for granted; they demanded it as their right.

Slowly she calmed down. Why blame Jean more than the others? It was the decadent atmosphere on the Island, living in the past, without pride, with no thought for tomorrow.

'It's sweet of you, Jean,' she managed to say lightly, 'but I've made my decision. I will marry Henry Revoir.'

Jean was still arguing about it as they reached the big wrought-iron gates. The little Creole girl came and bobbed and smiled as Annette smiled, and Annette looked at the scene before her, for the first time with the knowledge that she was to be its mistress.

Pierre, her father's servant, was working in the garden. He had wanted to be near her, and Henry, saying truthfully that Pierre was a little eccentric to fit in with the household staff, had suggested that he gardened. Now, as she looked at the neat, formal beds, the air of forlornness that she had noticed the first day, Annette began to plan. She would make that garden a picture with the calm lovely lagoon as its frame. She would have—

'The Chateau,' Jean said in a contemptuous voice. Pierre frowned. Already he was transferring his loyalties.

'And what is wrong with the Chateau, *monsieur?*' Pierre asked with perfect courtesy, but an obvious note of annoyance in his voice.

'What isn't?' Jean said, spreading his hands expressively. 'It requires painting and repairs inside. It is no place for a lovely young mistress.'

Pierre's eyes brightened. They asked Annette a question, and when she nodded, Pierre went on one knee and lifted Annette's

73

hand to his mouth.

'Your father would delight in the news, *messie,*' he said gravely. 'It would give him great happiness.'

A little embarrassed but touched by his obvious sincerity, Annette watched him stand up. A big man, he moved stiffly these days, as if the strength he needed while her father was alive had left him now it was no longer necessary. Annette turned to Jean, trying not to lose her temper.

'The Seigneur has many expenses,' she said with an unusual formality.

Jean scowled. 'So had *le Colonel,* but "Himself" is mean.'

Annette's nails dug into her flesh. She was unaware that from the Chateau, Henry Revoir was looking at them, unable to hear what they were saying, but noting the anger both were showing, Annette's more restrained than Jean's

'He is not mean,' she said, her voice shaking.

He glanced at her. 'He has great wealth.' Stiffly he bowed. 'I am desolate, but I must leave you now.' His hand on his heart. 'It is the great blow that I have received today.'

'Oh, Jean, be serious,' she said, her anger dissolving into laughter and seeing with relief that Jean's eyes were twinkling now. So it *was* a joke. With a slightly regal gesture she extended her hand and allowed him to kiss it.

'Thank you for walking home with me.'

'The pleasure was entirely mine,' Jean said, and turned away.

As Annette crossed the central lawn to the front door she felt gay and lighthearted. Her decision was made, for better or worse; but she had made it. Now she would have a cool shower, then a little rest on her bed, and it would be dinner time, the gracious leisurely meal she enjoyed most of all, and then Madame Lascie, giving her gentle vague smile, would leave them and—

As she entered the hall one of the doors opened and Henry was standing there staring at her. She knew a moment's unease. Had he seen her with Jean? He was looking angry. She stifled a sigh. It would have been hard enough normally to bring up the matter. Now it was far, far worse.

'Henry,' she began nervously.

'You should wear a hat,' he said crossly.

'I—I had a sunshade,' she said, showing him the pink one he had not noticed.

'You're mad to walk in this heat. You could have had the car.'

She coloured. 'I—I thought you wanted it.' She never would have the courage just to *take* the car; just to tell the chauffeur where to go.

He stood before her like a solid rock, a towering mountain.

'What did you want to ask me?'

Her eyes wavered. 'I forget,' she said. As

her eyes widened and she lifted her hand to her mouth in the little nervous way she had, he stepped aside.

He watched her almost scuttle up the stairs as if she could not get away fast enough.

It took all of Annette's courage to sit through the dinner and talk as if nothing had happened, or as if nothing was going to happen. She kept stealing little glances at the big, handsome man at the table. Was he really to be her husband? Until death do us part? In sickness and in health? She shivered.

Madame Lascie looked at her worriedly. 'You have caught the chill?'

'Too much sun, I should think,' Henry said, for Annette gave him a quick, guilty look. 'Your father could never get used to the sunshine.'

Silence fell heavily on the table. Madame Lascie battled politely to get the conversation going again. Annette was wondering again if she had made the right decision. She could go back to England, find a job. It was not that she feared poverty or work. She looked at Henry again and her heart seemed to turn over. The truth was that she could not bear to go away, knowing she would never see him again.

Her moment came later that evening when she was alone with Henry, and he was filling her liqueur glass. They had both sat silently gazing awkwardly into space. How was she going to start? It had to be faced.

She put down her glass and stood up, standing before him with her hands clasped behind her back, her face pale. Her eyes met his unwaveringly as she said:

'You were good enough to ask me to be your wife.' She paused for he had sat up, his eyes suddenly bright as he stared at her. 'Henri—'

At moments of emotion she found it easier to speak French and this name came more easily than the English word, *Henry.* 'My answer is yes.' As she spoke those irrevocable words her throat seemed to close so that her voice sounded squeaky. She hoped it would not sound so to him.

He stood up slowly. His hands touched her shoulders lightly as he bent and kissed her cheek.

'Thank you, Annette,' he said slowly. 'I will do my best to see that you never regret the decision.'

She stared at him sadly. For one wonderful moment she had hoped he was going to take her in his arms. The disappointment was a bitter one. As his hands released her she turned away hastily, hoping he would not see that her eyes were filled with tears as she hurried from the room.

All he had to do was to love her. Was that, then, too much to ask? she wondered as she hurried up to her bedroom and the joy of being alone, being able to give way to her fears. Had she made the mistake of her life? If only she knew!

CHAPTER SIX

In the morning, Annette awoke with a sense of excitement. Lying in bed, watching the long fingers of sunshine on the floor, she remembered that she was going to marry Henry Revoir. Her decision was made, she had told Henry; now they would start a new life together, partners.

She dressed swiftly and ran down through the garden to the steps that led to the lagoon. She perched herself on a rock and clasped her knees, delighting in the early sunshine, gazing down in the water at the small vividly coloured fishes.

Now that she had decided, she had a goal to work for: Henry's happiness. She would do all in her power never to let him regret the marriage. If she showed him that she could be a wonderful wife, if he came to lean on her— Her laughter rang out like a silver bell as she sat there in a backless pink frock, the gentle sea breeze blowing her dark hair over her face.

'Annette,' Henry said gently, and she turned her head and saw on his face such kindliness that she could not be afraid.

'Isn't it a heavenly morning?' she said

eagerly.

He came to sit by her side, to admire the blue of the lagoon, the cloudless sky, the palm trees with their feathery fronds.

'What were you thinking about?' he asked her.

She turned to him and he saw how long and curling were her lashes, how honest her eyes.

'You,' she told him.

He smiled. 'What about me?'

'I was wondering about your hobbies and interests,' she said gravely. 'A good wife shares her husband's interests.'

'Well, let's see.' He spoke with equal gravity. 'I'm very keen on golf. I like riding, deep sea fishing, yachting. I like music—good music.' He looked at her eager young face. 'I don't mean I don't like light music too,' he added.

'Dancing?' she asked him.

He grimaced. 'Depends on the person you're dancing with.' Suddenly he was laughing. 'But that applies to everything, doesn't it?' He looked at his watch. 'I don't want to be late for breakfast, Annette, as I have an important meeting this morning. May I—would you?' He hesitated a little. 'Have I your permission to announce our engagement?' he said formally. 'It is a matter of interest to the Islanders, of course.'

He stood up, pulling her to her feet. The thrill of his fingers as he touched her hands seemed to shoot right through her. She was

79

quite breathless as she answered, her cheeks rosy.

'Of course, Henry. I leave the announcement to you.'

She was quiet and thoughtful during breakfast as she and Madame Lascie enjoyed crisp freshly-made rolls while Henry worked his way through iced grapefruit, sausages, eggs and bacon and two pieces of toast and marmalade. What an appetite the man had, and how very good-looking he was, and how nice when he wasn't being angry. She found courage and said to him.

'I think I could start with golf, Henry. I would like to play with you.'

'You would like lessons?' he asked gravely.

Annette coloured, seeing but not knowing the reason for his amusement. 'Couldn't—you teach me?'

He considered the small pleading face for a moment. As he hesitated, the footman whisked away his empty plate and refilled his coffee cup. There was disappointment on Annette's face as she obviously thought his hesitation meant refusal.

'Of course I could,' he said. 'The course here is excellent, for it has many natural hazards you will never meet elsewhere,' he smiled ruefully. 'I'll send away for some clubs for you and you can get suitable shoes at Dominguez, and clothes.'

'I will advise Mademoiselle Laleham,'

80

Madame Lascie said quietly.

After Henry had left them, Annette escorted Madame Lascie to her favourite chair on the terrace. The lagoon was still as still could be, not a ripple showing. The heat of the sun-kissed land was already overwhelming. Madame Lascie began to fan herself as she smiled at Annette.

Annette's thoughts were far away. Henry would teach her to play golf. They would be together for hours, alone, walking and talking, and that would lay a foundation. Oh, how she would practise. She would work until he was proud of her.

'My dear child,' Madame Lascie said softly. 'I am so happy that you have made your decision. Monsieur Revoir told me of it, and I am glad. I am sure it is something you will never regret.'

Annette turned to her. 'Oh, I do hope not, Madame Lascie. I want to make him happy.'

'Ah,' Madame Lascie said as she looked affectionately at her charge, 'would that all wives thought of their husbands' happiness. I am sure you will. He is a fortunate man.'

'I want to learn to ride as well,' Annette said as she clasped her hands behind her head and gazed out at the garden—all hers—no, all *theirs*. That sounded much nicer.

'I have a friend, one Conrad Joseen. He has a riding school up in the mountains. If you wish it can be arranged with him to send down a good horse and a groom to teach you,' Madame Lascie suggested.

Annette turned to her excitedly. 'That would be wonderful.' Then her face fell. 'Clothes!'

Madame Lascie laughed. 'That also can be arranged. Dominguez" will send what we require on approval. You must be perfectly garbed—but perfectly.'

Annette sprang to her feet. 'Will you excuse me, *chère Madame,* if I leave you? I must also make an arrangement whereby I learn to fish and to sail.' She pulled a wry face. 'I hope I won't be seasick.'

Madame Lascie shrugged. 'Of what matter? In the pharmacy can be purchased pills.'

Annette smiled. 'You think of everything, Madame Lascie.'

She went to her bedroom and put on a thin voile frock. She looked round the bedroom with new eyes. Now that she was to be mistress and this was to be her home she could criticize. Mentally, of course. It was all clean, but something was lacking. Perhaps, as Henry had said, it was a woman's hand. She walked down the curving staircase thoughtfully, noticing the worn patches in the carpet, seeing that part of one of the chandeliers was missing. It was true that there was much to be done, but need it be done expensively? Madame Lascie had told her that in the attics were great trunks of discarded curtains and covers; that in the past some of the Revoir women had been wilfully extravagant, that much that had been tossed carelessly away into forgotten storage could be rescued and used.

One day she, Rennie and Madame Lascie would go to those attics and unpack those trunks. It would be wonderful fun. A lot of the painting she and Henry could do themselves.

She paused near the bottom stair, faltering a moment both in thoughts and footsteps. Somehow she could not see Henry on a ladder painting a picture rail. Well, she would get Jean to help her. He would do anything.

Jean Casca was in. He gave an ironic smile when she made her request.

'So—it is like an Austrian operetta? The rejected suitor is to teach his beloved how to become the person his rival desires,' he said.

'Jean, please be serious,' Annette said, sitting on the low wall outside his mother's house, grateful for the shade of the massive bougainvillaea that sprawled over the veranda. She felt very gay and happy, swinging her long slim legs, laughing up into Jean's dark eyes. 'You don't really love me.'

Jean put his hand on his heart. 'How cruel can you be? *Je t'adore.*'

Madame Casca came out of the little house. She frowned for a moment.

'Jean, it is not good that you make the jokes about love—and no more to Annette. You must remember now that she is the Seigneur's affianced wife. It is not seemly to behave so,' she said sternly.

'Oh, Madame Casca,' Annette cried. 'Please don't treat me any differently.'

The older woman looked at her. 'I'm afraid we will have to, *petite.* You *will* be different.' She turned back into the house.

Jean pulled a rueful face. 'You see, Annette? No more must I make the joke or pull the leg. You are now *someone,*' and he began to chuckle and soon Annette was joining in.

'But you will teach me to swim and to sail?' she said when they had regained soberness, 'and to enjoy fishing?'

Madeleine drifted out of the house, her lovely lark hair floating loosely on her shoulders, her lustrous eyes amused as she yawned. Annette stared at her in admiration. Whatever Madeleine did, she still looked beautiful. She wore a clinging rose-coloured negligee It had a small pleated train and it seemed to add to her graceful movements.

'You really want to sail?' she asked, both amused and shocked. 'Me—I would not go out in a little boat for—' She shrugged expressively. 'In the lagoon all is pleasant, but out there,' she indicated the wild waves that were racing in towards land, 'these maniacs, they say that sailing in the lagoon is no sport. It must be dangerous to be fun. Men! They are beyond comprehension. No man would get me out there.'

A shadow crossed Annette's face. She had always been scared of the sea—or of big waves. And wasn't it true that there were sharks here?

She lifted her small, determined chin and smiled.

'One can grow used to anything,' she said gaily.

Madeleine leant against the wall by her side. 'Tell me, little one,' she began in a lightly teasing voice, 'how is it that suddenly you wish to play golf, to ride, to sail?' Her eyes were shrewd as she looked at Annette's face. 'Is it because you wish to please "Himself?"' She nodded as Annette's startled, half-ashamed expression gave her away. 'It is a good thought, but—'

'It is not a good thought,' Jean said almost explosively. 'It is all wrong. You must make him your slave, Annette. He must dance to please you, he must learn to.' He paused and frowned 'What sort of things do *you* like doing, Annette?"

Her dimples appeared. 'I like to look at the sun, to read books, to listen to music.' She ticked the items off on her fingers as she spoke 'and I like to sew,' she added, her eyes dancing as she looked at his horrified face.

'Nom de dieu!' he cried, throwing his hands up in horror. 'Somehow I cannot see "Himself" *sewing!'*

They were all rocking with laughter when

85

shadow fell over them. They looked up and silence fell. Annette could feel the blood draining from her face as she stared at Henry.

'Henri—' she began, going to meet him

As he stood on the veranda, she thought how he towered above Jean. How shallow and insigificant Jean seemed beside the tall, impressive looking Henry Revoir. But Henry was not looking it her. He was obviously very angry about something. His face stern, two thin white lines by his mouth showed as he addressed Jean.

'I understand your roof is leaking again Could I see it?' He glanced at Madeleine and there vas something odd in his eyes, Annette thought. *'Bonjour,* or should I say good afternoon?' he said, his gaze flicking over the lovely girl and neeting her provocative glance.

Madeleine moved towards him with a stealthy feline movement.

'Ah, Henri.' Her voice was soft and reproachful. 'You know that I am what you call a lazee baggage, but must you point it out to me each time we meet?' She turned to Annette and her eyes were twinkling 'This so well-behaved english child, this fiancee of yours, she accepts me as as I am. She is not like you, Henri, always trying to reform us.' The voice was soft, but it seemed to Annette that there was a sting in the words.

Henry looked as if he thought so too. He began to speak and then closed his mouth firmly, turning to Jean expectantly and following him into the house.

Annette stood very still, cold and shivering. Why had he ignored her—insulted her, snubbed her in front of the others? Why was he so angry? And why with her?

Madeleine was laughing. 'What a one that man is, my poor Annette. Why cannot he relax and enjoy life? Why must he always be the reformer?' She shrugged. 'Life is too short, too sweet. So let us live as we like.'

Annette hesitated. She felt humiliated. And somehow there was a problem here that seemed to have no answer. Henry was right in trying to improve the Islanders if they made it impossible otherwise, for him to help them. Yet wasn't it smug of Henry to think that everyone save himself was wrong?

Suddenly she remembered that they had been talking of Henry—laughing at the thought of Henry sewing—when he interrupted them. Had Henry heard? Or had he just heard his name and thought they were laughing at him? Had he been hurt?

She wished she knew. She stifled the impulse to hurry after him, to explain. But he might look at her with those cold eyes of his, might snub her in front of the Cascas. With a man like Henri there was no telling what he would do.

'I must go,' she murmured. 'Please explain to your mother.' She hurried away and walked up the steep hill towards her father's *campentent.*

The sun blazed down. This time she had forgotten both hat and sunshade. Henry would be vexed.

As she walked into the garden, the parakeets screeched their usual welcome—if welcome it was meant to be. Annette stood on the small veranda and thought of the hours of happiness she had spent there with her father. If only—!

If only Henry had not arrived at that moment of laughter with the Cascas. She would hate to have him think they were mocking him. The hostility on the Island could have made him sensitive. It was not fair, a good man like that. He seemed so sure of himself—so self-contained, but his face when Madeleine had teased him had betrayed his inner feelings. If only she knew how to help him. If only she need not always make him so angry.

Leaning against one of the pillars, her eyes closed, Annette did not hear the car stopping, and it was only the screeching of the parakeets that made her open her eyes. Henry was standing there staring at her, his face blank. Oh please God, she found herself praying silently, please show me the way to help him without hurting him.

'Henri,' she said softly, and was quite unaware that she was holding out her hands to him. 'Henri—isn't it all beautiful?'

He moved forwards towards her and took her hands. 'Beautiful,' he said.

Her fingers curled round his and for a moment she allowed herself to hope. She looked up at the face that had such a strange smile and wished with all her heart that she dared to tell him the truth, that she loved him to despair, and ask him couldn't he learn to love her? But how did you tell a man that? How could you?

She spoke aloud. 'Henri—will you—would you?'

He dropped her hands abruptly. 'What is it you want?' he asked harshly.

She caught her breath, her small white teeth biting into her lower lip painfully. What had she done to anger him? What had happened to that brief but wonderful moment? It made her stutter as she asked:

'I w-wondered if you had t-time to teach me to drive?'

'I have time now,' he said curtly.

Trembling with excitement, Annette sat by his side in the long, low cream car trying to concentrate as he explained the different gears, then the instruments on the panel of the dashboard It was hard to concentrate. If only she was not made so breathless because of his nearness. Then there was her anxiety about the little scene at the Cascas'; she kept trying to phrase and rephrase tactful explanations of the reason for their laughter. Yet it seemed impossible to mention it without either hurting him, or even perhaps annoying him by the implication that it *might* have hurt him. Oh dear, what a very very difficult man he was, to be sure. His moods changed like the colours on the sun-kissed sea.

Now he was being quite friendly.

'I've told you ten times,' he said patiently, his hand closing over hers as he guided her through the gears.

'I'm sorry.' She looked at him apologetically. 'I wasn't listening.'

'Why on earth not?' For a moment he was stern. 'Do you really want to learn?'

'It's the gears,' Annette told him humbly. 'I have driven my aunt's car, but it was a very old one. The gears then were on the floor.'

'So you *can* drive?' Henry demanded.

She looked at him. 'If you can call that driving. I would just go down the lanes to the station, to the post office or the shops. It was perhaps three miles away. I was not allowed the car for pleasure and—and you had to drive slowly or things fell out.'

'Not you, I hope,' he said with a smile.

'I nearly did once. It happened—' Annette relaxed as she told him about the time she had forgotten to bang the door of the car and rounding a corner had found herself leaning outside the car, clinging to the steering wheel for dear life. When Henry laughed she felt happier, and when he suggested driving her to a wide suitable part of the road, she sat contentedly by his side, stealing glances at his face.

How could he guess the disturbing effect his closeness had on her? The tangy whiff of eau-de-cologne combined with the masculine fragrance of the tobacco he smoked had her trembling. When his hand covered hers, or his shoulder brushed against her, it was difficult to concentrate on the car.

An hour later, he took her back to the Chateau. 'You soon picked it up,' he said approvingly. 'Two more lessons and you can drive the car alone.'

Her hand flew to her throat. 'Oh, Henri—may I? Thank you.' She smiled at him, but she felt exhausted, drained by the happiness she had known. Now she felt that it *might* be possible for them to find real happiness in their marriage, by sharing things or if he would teach her. 'You are so patient.'

'Patient?' Henry laughed. 'Tell that to the Islanders.'

She hesitated. 'They will learn in time.'

He lifted his eyebrows quizzically. 'You talk like your father. Have I enough time?'

Impulsively she laid her hand lightly on his. 'We'll make it enough time,' she promised softly and slid out of the car and into the Chateau, for Henry had told her he would not be coming in nor would he be in until late that

91

evening as he had affairs to settle.

Annette found Madame Lascie nodding over her embroidery and she kissed her thin veined hand affectionately.

'Ah,' Madame said, and smiled. 'You have had a morning of the happiest?'

'Indeed I have,' Annette said, pulling a chair closer, looking round Madame Lascie's sitting-room thoughtfully. A pretty room, it was built with three walls only, and the window was high up so that you could not see the lagoon, nor the ocean beyond it, nor the waving palm trees. Here you were in a little world of your own. Maybe when they were married she would make this her little sanctuary, a place to come to when things got difficult. For they would; even the happiness she felt at that moment did not delude her.

She told Madame Lascie about the driving lesson. 'I must make myself the kind of wife of whom Henri can be proud,' Annette said, and looked shyly at her companion. 'Jean says I am a fool, that I should make Henri my slave, but I—'

Madame Lascie laid her hand lightly on Annette's dark curls. 'You are the one who is right, my child.'

Annette always felt happiest conversing in French with Madame Lascie, just as she did with the Cascas. 'It is the woman who sets the rhythm if the marriage,' Madame continued. 'If you work to make your husband happy,

92

then you will find happiness also. A selfish desire it is to have a slave, but that,' she paused and shrugged, 'that was always Madeleine's trouble. That was how she lost—' Madame paused, her hands trembling as she folded her needlework. 'Would it not be pleasant to have some coffee, child? Would you be so good as to ring the bell for me?'

Annette obeyed, pulling on the old-fashioned bell-rope in the corner. Why had Madame Lascie hesitated?

'I've always wondered what was Madeleine's tragedy,' she said.

Madame Lascie looked disturbed. 'Ah, but that—well, she made a great muchness out of a pitiable little,' Madame was saying when the coffee arrived, and her hands fluttered almost like frightened swallows as she arranged the cups. 'It is not good to talk of it, and one day she will tell you.'

Seeing Madame's real distress, Annette changed the subject, but she often wondered what man it was who could resist Madeleine, who was so lovely, so provocative.

On Madame's advice, Annette became the possessor of white cotton riding breeches, Some long shining boots, an elegantly cut coat, shirts. She also chose a divided skirt for golf of the most delightful shade of bluebell blue. She enjoyed her riding lessons. She also spent happy hours on the small golf course, set out on the mountains high above the hot

93

steaming valley, with the most heavenly views when she paused to gaze out over the ocean at the dim haze that hid the other islands. Fortunately she learned quickly, or Henry was a good instructor, but never once did he become vexed with her on the golf course. She swam with Jean and Madeleine, had her first sailing trip, making Jean promise he would not go out far. As she sat clutching the sides of the small boat, leaning as Jean directed her, the spray dancing up into her face, the huge waves tossing them about she found her fear going. At first she watched the water anxiously, looking for a slim grey shape that would be a shark. But gradually she began to enjoy it, to come back with her hair ruffled by the wind, her cheeks rosy and sunburned, filled with a great contentment. But she discovered that Henry did not approve of her outings with the Cascas.

'Why should that be so?' Annette asked Madame Lascie worriedly, one day. 'Always he is cross when I have been with them.'

Madame Lascie hid a smile. 'It could be that he is jealous,' she suggested quietly.

'Jealous?' Annette said, her eyes widening with amazement. 'Do you think so?'

She went away hugging the suggestion to her heart. Could Henry be jealous? If so, that meant—

After that she stayed away from the Cascas as much as she could, and when she went with

94

them she did not mention it to Henry. Nor did he ask her what she had been doing. He seemed content to drift as they were doing. Sometimes she wondered when they would marry.

Madame Lascie had a suggestion about this also. 'It is possible that he wishes you to lose your fear of him.' She nodded her head in answer to Annette's startled look. 'It is plain that you are terrified of him.'

'Only when he is angry,' Annette said, horrified that she had betrayed herself.

'He has much to make him angry,' Madame Lascie said sadly.

It was strange, Annette thought, as she strolled about the garden, talking to Pierre, planning to have a rose garden here, a small pool there—but the Cascas had shut up like clams about the Islanders and their troubles, ever since the engagement was announced. It showed great delicacy of thought, but she hoped her new position as Henry Revoir's wife was not going to erect a barrier between herself and the Islanders. If it did, it would make her plans to help Henri impossible to carry out.

Often, now that she was allowed to drive the car, Annette would drive to one or other of the small towns. She loved to park the car and wander through the narrow crowded streets, brushing shoulders with the strangest conglomeration of human beings she had ever seen. Chinese coolies running along the cobbled streets, dancing about with their little two-wheeled carts behind them—dark-faced men in red fezes and long flowing white robes, the *Malagazy* natives with their white lmbas and their huge raffia palm-leaf hats. Henry had told her once that the size of the hat or rather the width of the brim was a sign of wealth. There was much to hate in the town; poverty showing in the small bare piccaninnies playing in the gutters, a glimpse of a sullen face as a woman walked by, her *lamba* torn and dirty, her hands like claws as she held them out, begging in a whining voice.

Dominguez was a shop that catered for all, but the proprietor himself pushed his way through the crowds when he saw Annette. He came bowing, rubbing his hands, smiling at her. Only because she was a good customer, she thought, as he led her through the noisy, smelly crowd to a back room and seated her, producing a bottle of wine and two glasses, and then she was ashamed. She was catching Henry's cynical habits and she did not want to do so.

It made her a little self-conscious, perhaps stiffened her voice. She was greatly concerned, and had been for some time, with the thought of her trousseau. She felt strongly that the girl's family or, if she had no parents, the girl herself, should buy the trousseau. But what with? as Madame Lascie had, with the

96

practical common sense of the French, pointed out. So Annette decided to make as much of the trousseau herself, as she could. Later, when she was Henry's wife, she would have no sense of shame when she spent his money on her clothes.

Dominguez listened to her desires and brought out roll after roll of exquisite silk, the loveliest pastel shades. The price shocked her.

'I could not afford that,' she said.

Dominguez flung his hands up in horror. 'The Seigneur can afford it, Mademoiselle. He is not a poor man.'

Annette frowned. The small room was hot and stuffy, the wine had given her a headache. Her fingers fondled the lovely soft material. It would wear for ages and wash beautifully. Perhaps it was not an extravagance.

Dominguez took charge of the situation. 'The Seigneur has an account with us, *naturellement*. You wish for the pink, the cream, the blue, the green.'

Annette began to laugh. 'Wait,' she said. Dominguez's eager hands halted as he stopped measuring the material. 'The Seigneur is not a poor man, but he has many expenses. I will take the pink and the green.'

Dominguez also had a sewing machine he thought she might like. 'But of the newest, of course.' He looked at her curiously. 'Mademoiselle will make her own trousseau?' He sounded disapproving.

'But of course,' Annette said. 'Most of it I shall stitch by hand.'

She sailed out of the shop, thinking of the happy hours that lay ahead of her. The material was beautiful, so soft, so—

Everywhere she went along the twisting narrow road with the deep shadows and the blinding patches of sunlight and the queer almost sinister alleys, Annette was met by smiles and bows.

'I felt like royalty, bowing all the time,' she laughingly told Madame Lascie when she returned to the Chateau.

Madame Lascie smiled placidly. 'But you are. To us the Revoirs *are* our Royal Family.'

Undoing the parcels that had been delivered with amazing speed, Annette showed her chaperone the lovely material; she was glad that Madame Lascie approved her purchases.

'It is a big responsibility,' Annette said slowly, 'to be looked on like that. It means—'

'That every eye is watching you, all the time,' Madame Lascie said slowly, watching the grave young face anxiously. 'You must always act with the greatest discretion. Your remarks will be repeated, often distorted, so you must not be hurt if sometimes people are offended. Then—' She hesitated. 'Then you will have a great influence over your husband and so many will try to make you their—how do you say it?—their tool.'

Annette sat back on her heels, rubbing a

tired hand over her eyes, her happiness gone. 'You mean—' she said slowly. She looked up and for a moment her face lost the look of youth. 'You mean that they may try to make me persuade Henri to do the things they want him to do?'

'But of course. It is a temptation too great to be withstood,' Madame Lascie said sadly. 'But have no fears, you will make the Seigneur a good wife,' she nodded, her small head moving like a little china mandarin's.

'It won't be easy,' Annette said, slowly rising, gathering up the material, wondering why she suddenly felt desolate.

'Nothing is easy,' Madame said softly. 'Just be prepared for anything and never show your dismay.'

That was advice that should be easy enough to follow, Annette thought ruefully as she went downstairs later that day carrying the material, but with a difficult man like Henry—'

How right she was! Next morning as she sat in the cool little room, almost an annexe of the great impressive-looking drawing-room with french windows wide open, the light filtering in through the leaves of the young trees planted just outside, she remembered her thoughts. There was a small chaise-longue that she had placed so that she could curl up on it and look out at the garden and the deep blue of the water beyond. She hummed as she stitched the seams of the silk petticoat she was making.

Every now and then she stopped to admire her tiny stitches.

Suddenly the door burst open and there was Henry Revoir. She looked up with her swift happy smile, but it vanished as she saw the well-known thin white lines on either side of his mouth. He was wearing immaculate white shorts with a thin white silk shirt and rope-soled shoes on his bare feet. Was he going sailing? Was he going to ask her to go with him?

'What exactly are you doing?' he demanded, his voice shaking.

She sat up abruptly, jerking the needle, pricking her finger so that it bled. Like a frightened child, she sucked the finger, gazing up at him, her eyes huge.

'M-making a petticoat,' she mumbled through her fingers, 'for my trousseau,' she added, her voice softening. Someone had vexed him. Now she saw that she had vexed him still more.

He shut the door with a quick, impatient movement. He was trembling with anger.

'Look,' he said with an ominous quietness. 'I am neither a millionaire nor a poor man. You insult me when you let the Islanders know you have to sew your own trousseau.'

'I—I like hand-sewn clothes,' Annette tried to say, but he was not listening.

'We'll have no more of this—this ridiculous nonsense. I am flying to Durban next week

100

on business. You and Madame Casca will accompany me and she can assist you in buying a trousseau.'

'Durban?' Annette breathed. She had heard so much about that South African city with the lovely shops and tall white skyscrapers, the beautiful Valley of a Thousand Hills, the lovely cliffs and beaches. 'But—'

'I can afford our fares,' he said stiffly. 'I wish you would not harp on money. When I need you to plead poverty for me, I'll tell you— understand?' he went on savagely. 'I don't like it, whatever game it is that you're playing at— understand? I won't have you tell the Islanders I spend too much on them, that people should mend their own roofs.' He saw the tell-tale flush in her cheeks. 'You told young Casca that.'

Annette faced him. 'It's true.'

'It may be,' he said grimly. 'But you keep out of it. We'll go to Durban next week. You must have a trousseau suitable for your position,' he finished, stalking out of the room and slamming the door.

Slowly Annette folded up her needlework, looked through a mist of tears at the beautiful scene outside. His angry words clamoured like chattering magpies in her brain. He did not care about her. He did not mind if she even *liked* the trousseau. All that mattered was that she should have a trousseau suitable for her position.

She buried her face in her hands as the tears took over. How could she ever hope to make him happy or be happy with him when the slightest thing she did could act like a boomerang?

When the tears had gone she dried her eyes and tried to plan. In Durban it would be easier to get a job. In Durban she would tell him the truth. That she knew they could never make a success of this marriage, that it was all a farce. Most Frenchwomen preferred handmade undies, but then there was so little French about Henry that maybe he could not be expected to understand. Perhaps that was the trouble.

She stood up, feeling stiff and exhausted. In Durban she would tell him the truth. That she could not marry him after all.

CHAPTER SEVEN

As the days passed, neither Annette nor Henry referred to the little scene, but she felt there was tension in the air. Often she caught him staring at her with a puzzled look, and she longed to fling herself in his arms and tell him there was nothing to wonder about, that she loved him with all her heart.

The day he mentioned his mother, Annette had a distinct shock. She had heard so much of the second Madame Revoir; of how she hated the Island, refused to live there, separated Henry from his father, took Henry to America when the war began, and with no reason for it, had somehow imagined that Henry's mother was dead. Henry had found Annette in the garden where she was discussing with Pierre the sadly neglected grass tennis court. Pierre's dark eyes watched her with almost slavish devotion as he nodded his head wisely. When Henry joined them, Annette turned to him nervously. Since that unpleasant little scene she had been afraid to suggest repairs or improvements to the house, for she dared not mention economical methods nor suggest expensive alterations . . . Whatever she did could be wrong.

'Henri, it would be nice to play tennis. I'm not bad. And—and then there's that summerhouse—' She indicated a rather ornate but terribly dilapidated summer-house built on a small incline, facing the tennis court and the lagoon. 'It would be so nice for informal tea parties.'

'It shall be repaired,' he promised her. 'I want to talk to you,' he continued stiffly.

Nervously she went to sit with him on a curved wrought-iron seat below a riotously luxuriant flamboyant tree.

'I've sent a cable to my mother,' he told her curtly.

Annette fought back dismay. How could she

have forgotten his mother?

'Will—will she mind?' she asked.

Henry frowned. 'Why should she mind?' he asked. 'I'm not a child.'

'You are *her* child,' Annette said, giving him a curious look. She felt confused, unable to sort out her thoughts—a state she was in most of the time; one moment planning for their future together, loving the Chateau, learning from Madame Lascie how to run a large staff such as this, learning about the right procedure at formal dinner parties; the next moment making up her mind—only to change it again—that in Durban she would tell Henry she could not marry him. He was just like the little girl in the nursery rhyme: *When he was nice, he was very, very nice, but when he was bad, he was horrid!* 'She may think me too young,' Annette went on. 'She may have other ideas for you.'

Henry laughed at that. 'She has—but they don't include matrimony. Don't worry,' he went on, looking up and surprising the dismay on Annette's face. 'She will accept the fact that we're to be married, but I must tell her, for she will want to come to our wedding.'

Our wedding.

He said the words so casually. She looked at the tall, broad-shouldered, handsome man as he sat staring with a frown at Pierre, who was bent over some flowers in a bed. She dared not think of their wedding. How could she marry

104

him, deliberately walking into heartache? Yet if she walked out of his life—

'Don't worry, Annette,' Henry said again his voice kind as he looked into her surprised eyes. 'She'll like you all right.' His mouth wa suddenly grim. 'Don't wait dinner for me, I may be late,' he said curtly, and walked off.

Annette felt stifled as she sat there. What would Henry's mother be like? The Islanders had caller her cold, a snob, inhuman, selfish.

She stood up, leaving the shelter of the tree for the blinding heat of the sun. She would spew the rest of the day with the Cascas. Jean would take her swimming, maybe lend her those goggles and flippers again, and they would look at those thrilling tiny undersea flowers, and in this way she could forget Henry's mother for a little while.

Jean was glad to see her. As they ran down towards the sands, he asked her when she was going to Durban.

'Three days' time,' Annette said.

'I wish I could go with you.' Jean's face was sullen.

Annette could laugh, feeling her misery lighten. 'I don't know what Henri would say,' she cried gaily.

'I can imagine,' Jean told her, scowling and then beginning to laugh as they reached the water coming racing towards them. 'We'll walk along the sands to the lagoon,' he told her, his eyes warm and admiring.

For a moment she wondered if she was being fair to him, but the next moment the fear subsided. Jean was not the sort of man to become serious. There was no danger of hurting him or of breaking his heart.

As they walked through the warm sea, letting the waves break against their legs, curl round their toes, he told her about Durban and what she must do and see.

Three days later Annette, Henry and Madame Casca left the Island. Madame Casca made Annette feel like a country bumpkin in her cotton frock and darned gloves, for she wore a black shantung suit, a minute hat tilted over her eyes and impeccable gloves and shoes. Henry was quiet as he helped them fasten their belts and left them to sit alone. Annette wished he was with her, but he had a pile of papers he was checking, his face absorbed and anxious.

At Durban he took Madame Casca and Annette to a huge white hotel on the front, apologizing for leaving them, but he had many people to see, he arranged to have dinner with them that evening.

Madame Casca beamed. 'This is a lovely task he has given me,' she told Annette happily. 'The trousseau to buy—money unlimited. Ah, first we will have the rest and then take the stroll and look at the shops and tomorrow—ah, tomorrow we will start to make the purchases.'

Durban was a lovely town. She had seen so little of the world; first the quiet Somersetshire village and then the Island. It was fascinating to walk down the wide streets and to gaze into the huge windows filled with lovely clothes. The sunshine poured down, but there were alway arcades where there was shade. It was fun, too, going to the cinema, for in England she had only seen those films that had been shown at the school and sometimes one in the village. Now she was seeing the latest type of film, huge screens, wonderful incredible colours, famous stars of whom she had read.

Then at night they always went to a different restaurant with Henry, sometimes there would be what he called a 'floor-show'; a dancer or a singer, often from Europe. But always there was one snag to all the wonders of it—Annette was never alone with Henry.

He was quite right, of course. He did it for her sake, making certain that they were always chaperoned, but it irked Annette, for it raised a barrier of formality between them. She began to wish their visit was over, to long for the quietness of the Chateau where Madame Lascie went out of her way to leave the young couple alone as much as possible.

It was thrilling, though, to buy the trousseau. That first night Annette had made herself face the truth. She had thought a lot of nonsense, but never once had she really meant to tell Henry she could not marry him.

She knew in her heart that she could never—ever—give up the chance of marrying Henry. At least, as his wife, she had the opportunity to make him love her, an opportunity that would not be hers if she shut herself out of his life.

So she could choose the trousseau with a clear conscience. Madame Casca was a wonderful companion, but so ruthless at times that often Annette whispered an apology to offended sales ladies whose choice had been ridiculed, whose taste had been torn to bits.

'But what an absurdity,' Madame Casca would cry in a horrified voice. *'Une jeune fille* like Mademoiselle and you produce *that!'* She would touch the frock with a finger that screamed disgust. 'Pshaw! Remove it at once.'

Slowly, excitingly, Annette's wardrobe grew. It was amazing how many clothes she needed; a suit for chilly days—this for when she travelled with 'Himself', Madame said firmly. Annette's heart seemed to skip a beat—travel with Henry! Perhaps he would take her to Paris? Venice—Rome? A fine tweed it was, made of a strange green colour that matched her silk blouse. The blouses were lovely, too, some tailored and of sheer silk; others softly pleated or with ruffles falling from the collar. A small hat of rainbow-hued feathers, a huge straw hat that cost so much Annette gasped, its sole ornamentation a minute bunch of violets under the brim. Sheath dresses, shirtwaister frocks; blue, green, pink; every colour but

108

black. Henry loathed black. Cocktail party frocks of a slim elegance made of rustling shot taffeta or heavy corded silk A navy blue frock with an enormous white collar; dinner frocks, elegant but with a quietness that revealed their cost. Two wonderful ball gowns; for Madame Casca said that when Annette was married she must renovate the ballroom and hold a ball, 'as it was done in days gone by,' she said nostalgically. 'In those days, the Chateau was always open to us. We were welcome as rain in the dry season.'

She laughed and shrugged. 'On Sundays we all went to play tennis and croquet—often we had a cold buffet luncheon. That was the first Madame Henri Revoir, the mother of Maurice; devoted to her husband, to the Island. She was so beautiful, so kind.'

Then there were undies in apricot, dusty pink, a pale lime green, a golden corn shade, diaphanous negligees. Annette wondered if she could ever trail round in one as Madeleine did so effectively. Shoes, high thin heels, medium and flat heels at her own insistence, sensible brogues for golf, rope-soled slippers for the beach. Was there no end to it?

Once she dared to say something to Henry and he lifted one eyebrow in surprise as he so often did. 'We will not be near the shops for at least six months. Your wardrobe must be sufficient,' he told her quite kindly

Six months! Surely her wardrobe would

last a lifetime? She spent hours when she was supposed to be resting or asleep, just gazing at the wonderful clothes, touching the materials. One ball gown had fifty yards of tulle in the enormous skirt, looped with deep crimson ribbon, each loop decorated with a small but exquisite bunch of roses. She tried it on, whirling round the room, her arms out, her face radiant. Would Henry dance with her?

White silk shirts, jodhpurs; flippers and goggles, three new swim suits, gay jeans and shirts, shorts and loose jackets. Once, a little intoxicated with the wonder of it all, she found courage to speak to Henry when they were momentarily alone.

'Henri,' she said softly, so softly that he had to put down his glass and lean towards the girl with the huge starry eyes, the trembling mouth. 'Please don't be vexed with me, but are you sure you can afford it?'

'I promise you I can afford it,' he said gravely.

'Oh, Henri,' she said from her heart.

One day Annette bought a book on how to play bridge. She tried to understand it, but it made the whole business of bridge sound such a nightmare. Surely you played cards for fun? Madame Lascie had said she should learn, that when they entertained they would need her to play bridge with the guests. 'He is very fond of bridge,' she had added, a twinkle in her eye, and Annette had known that somehow or other she must learn how to play.

Then came the wonderful day when Madame Casca was left at the hotel and Henry took Annette out alone. It was a perfect day, a perfect world, Annette thought excitedly as Henry handed her into the taxi and gave the driver directions.

'Look, Henri,' Annette said excitedly, pointing out a particularly resplendent rickshaw boy as he leapt into the air, whooping noisily, prancing as he pulled along the two-wheeled rickshaw in which two girls, obviously off one of the many ships in the docks, were clinging to each other and screaming with laughter. The rickshaw boy wore the usual garments, but this one was covered with beads, rows after rows of them, his headdress was made of two great curving horns and some wonderfully gay feathers. His black face was shining as he pranced along.

As she spoke, Henry looked down at her and noticed her white pleated frock which fitted perfectly and the black straw hat tipped over her eyes, the black handbag and gloves. She looked different, and yet her eyes were the same and so was her smile.

'You'll miss this,' he said abruptly as the taxi took them down Smith Street, stopping at a shop.

She looked at him, surprised. 'Oh, I wouldn't like to live here always. It's fun for a change, but I love the Island.' Her voice shook

111

as she spoke.

He frowned. 'It's not a good idea to grow too fond of a place. Look how long it took me to get over the shock of having to leave London, yet today, I couldn't go back to my old life. You must move forward and not live in the past. That's the trouble with the Islanders,' he told her gravely.

He took her to a very elegantly furnished room above a jeweller's shop. There they were greeted by a small man with white hair and a monocle. With much ceremony, he seated them in deep armchairs, pulled up a little table.

'Monsieur, I think I have just what you want. When you telephoned I was out, but—' He opened a drawer in the oval walnut table and produced a tray lined with black velvet. Reverently he laid it on the small table before Annette. She could not suppress her gasp of surprise. She had never seen such rings in all her life.

'Make your choice,' Henry said abruptly.

Some odd note in his voice made her look up. He had lost interest already, was strolling round gazing at the etchings on the walls. Some of her excitement died. The rings were lovely and expensive because the Seigneur's fiancée must have the best. It had nothing to do with Annette herself. Henry did not care.

She examined each ring in turn. One was a most beautiful square-cut emerald, the next an enormous diamond—sparkling and almost vulgar, she felt, in its ostentatiousness The third was lovely; four diamonds round a deep blue sapphire. It was hard to choose. And then she picked up the last one and knew that this would be her choice. It was an emerald, but much smaller than the first one; this was held by a beautifully carved setting in the shape of clasped hands.

'Mademoiselle should look inside,' the jeweller murmured in her ear. Obediently she turned the ring. She could see some writing, but could not read it, nor recognize the language It was not French.

'It says: *Until death us do part,*' he told her softly.

'This is the ring, please, Henri,' Annette said firmly. She slid it on her finger. It fitted perfectly. She slid it off again and laid it on the tray. It was his place to put the ring on her hand.

Henry stared at her, puzzled. 'I thought the emerald or the big diamond.'

'This one, please,' Annette said again, clasping her hands.

The little jeweller beamed. 'As soon as I saw Mademoiselle, I knew it was for her.'

'All right,' Henry said curtly.

While Henry went off into another room to settle details, the elderly Frenchman talked to Annette. 'It has a story, that ring, but yes. Several centuries ago it was designed and made for a young prince who was forced to make a marriage of convenience, a girl he hated—but he had no choice,' Monsieur Verabin continued. 'He gave this ring to his true love, and swore that she was his only love, that never would he love another one. She wore this ring until the day she died. She never saw the prince again and only knew that he had died before her. When she was buried, she asked for the ring to be buried with her, but alas, it was stolen. A century later, it was on the market. The thief was never traced ; it had been through too many hands.' He smiled. 'I hope that this time the ring will bring good fortune.'

Henry was waiting, looking impatient, saying as she followed him, 'You've left the ring behind.'

Blushing, she turned to the table and picked it up, sliding it on to her finger, looking up and seeing compassion in the elderly Frenchman's eyes. Henry should have put it on, she thought miserably.

In the taxi, Henry asked in an unusual voice, 'Are you sure it's the one you want, Annette? Quite, quite sure?'

She saw real anxiety in his eyes, knew he wanted to make her happy, and her resentment vanished. She smiled at him radiantly and on an impulse leant towards him, dropping a kiss lightly on his cheek.

'I love it, Henri. Very, very much.'

Before he could answer her, the taxi stopped outside the hotel. She almost ran indoors, eager to show Madame Casca her ring. Henry followed.

Madame Casca went into rhapsodies about the ring. Henry watched her unsmilingly. She had served his purpose. She would tell the Islanders of the money he had recklessly splashed on his future wife, and they would blame him for it just as they would blame him if he did the reverse and behaved like a miser. Nothing he could do was right.

Flying back to the Island in the plane, Annette closed her eyes and dreamed. It was going to be all right. Already she knew Henry better. When they were married she would gradually learn the things that displeased him and would be careful not to offend. Look how very kind he was—and generous. No one could have been more wonderful.

It would be good to be back in the Chateau with dear Madame Lascie smiling encouragingly at her, leaving them alone as much as she could. Now she would soon be able to ride with Henry, play golf with him, sail with him, and one day when she had mastered that difficult book, she would play bridge with him. It would be a good life.

It was a shock when, as the cream car reached the Chateau and Henry helped Annette out of the car, directing the chauffeur to take Madame Casca home, two women

115

came out of the front door, to stand on the terrace, staring at them.

They made no sign, did not speak. When Henry turned back from speaking to the chauffeur, he saw them.

He could not hide the dismay in his voice. 'Mother, I didn't expect you yet,' he exclaimed, and then his voice changed again as his eyes fell on the girl standing by his mother's side. 'Valda!'

Valda was beautiful. She was more than that. Striking—vivid—what words could describe her? Annette wondered, as her heart sank. Flaming red hair, swept up into a flat coil on top of her head, strangely grey eyes that were mocking everyone as she stood there, her lovely slim body clasped by a sea green frock.

'My dear Henry—when I heard the news I could not believe it,' she said in a husky, amused voice. 'I simply had to come and see with my own eyes. So this is the bride.' She stared at Annette rather as if she was looking at some strange object. 'A little young, surely?'

Henry's arm was round Annette's shoulder. For a moment her heart leapt with joy, but almost at once she recognized it for what it was—a gesture of defiance. 'Not too young, Valda,' Henri drawled.

'Don't you think so?' Valda mocked. 'Surely you must feel like a cradle-snatcher. I know I would, in your shoes.'

Henry's voice was amused as he replied,

116

'My dear Valda—you should know, seeing that we are the same age.'

It served Valda right, but all the same Annette felt sorry for her as she saw the colour come swiftly to Valda's cheeks, and the fury in her eyes. And then Henry was walking up the shallow steps, Annette walking with him, still conscious of his arm around her. She looked at Henry's mother, feeling it would be kinder not to go on staring at the discomfited Valda.

Henry's mother was a short but very thin woman with blue-white hair, dressed elaborately. She sparkled with diamonds—in her ears, on her fingers She had a pointed chin, a thin mouth and cool, appraising eyes as she watched them approach. She wore a very tight blue sheath frock and Annette wondered how she could breathe.

'Mother, this is Annette Laleham,' Henry said. Mrs. Revoir touched Annette's hand lightly, her fingers cold as ice. 'Are you serious, Henry?' Mrs. Revoir said, just as if Annette was not there by their side.

'Quite serious, Mother,' Henry replied. 'Never more serious in my life.' He sounded amused again. 'Let's go inside—we've had a tiring journey. I think a bath and a rest is in order, eh, Annette darling?'

The word of endearment should have thrilled her, but it had the reverse effect. As unobtrusively as she could, Annette slid away from Henry's arm and stood alone.

117

'It would be pleasant,' she said coolly, horribly aware that her nose must be shiny, her lips pale, her dress crumpled.

'I'm going for a walk,' Valda announced. 'Coming, Henry?'

Henry was looking at his mother as she stood a little to one side, her sharp nose jutting out in her face, her mouth a thin line of distaste.

'Would you care to join us, Mother?'

'It might be as well,' she said sourly. Her eyes slid slowly over Annette. 'We can talk later,' she said.

'You'll be all right, Annette?' Henry asked, his voice kind.

She lifted her head, tilting her chin 'But of course, Henry darling,' she said gaily. 'I'm longing for a bath, though. I'll see you later.'

She sailed into the house, having bestowed on them all a vaguely general smile, just getting indoors and out of sight in time before the foolish tears stung her eyes. So *that* was the girl he had loved, the girl whose ideas about life were completely different. He had not forgotten her. You could hear that in the way he spoke to her.

Her little Creole maid came hurrying to greet her, to help her undress, to escort her to the bathroom, to chatter away in her funny little voice but all the time Annette could only remember Valda—tall, perfectly proportioned, lovely, sophisticated, alive. All that Henry

118

could want.

When she was alone, Annette held the ring Henry had given her to her cheek. Once before had been worn by a woman whose heart must have broken. Was history going to repeat itself?

CHAPTER EIGHT

So began a new life; a different, a lonely life. The first thing Annette learned was that both Mrs. Revoir and Valda were quite ruthless. They were Annette's enemies and they would stop at nothing to prevent the marriage. It was not too bad when Henry was there. Valda was charming, Mrs. Revoir patient and condescending, but the instant he was gone—

She grew to dread those times alone in the great Chateau with her mother-in-law to be, and Valda. Annette had not a friend to turn to, for Madame Casca was not welcomed to the Chateau and Madame Lascie had been dismissed like a servant before Annette and Henry had returned from Durban.

'Madame Lascie?' Valda had said disdainfully. 'Of course we sent her packing. We didn't want her around, and with us here, there's no need for a chaperone. In any case, she's just another of these parasites.'

Annette had trembled as she controlled her

anger. 'I don't know what Henri will say,' she said.

Valda lifted her thin dark eyebrows. 'Say? He said nothing. Naturally we told him, and he agreed we had done the right thing,' she said smoothly.

Annette turned away. What was the good of arguing? She seized her first chance of going to see Madame Lascie in her small pink house sheltered by a cluster of casuarina trees. She was sitting on her small veranda, huddled under a blanket, her skin even more tautly drawn across her cheek bones.

'I am so sorry, Madame Lascie. I was so happy to have you with us in the Chateau,' Annette said as she kissed the ivory-coloured cheek. 'I hope—I hope they—' she hesitated. It was difficult to suggest that your future mother-in-law might have been discourteous.

'Do not worry, my child,' Madame Lasci reassured her. 'I have the understanding.' Her eyes twinkled as she added: 'Remember that it is the son you are going to marry and not his mother.'

Annette wondered. Over fragrant coffee and crisp biscuits she confessed her fears. 'I'm sure Henri is still in love with Valda. She makes me feel so young, so gauche. She always looks at me as if I amuse her and it makes me fumble and drop things.'

'But that is what she wants, and this you must not allow,' Madame Lascie said in a

120

firm voice, fanning herself with a delicately beautiful hand-painted fan. 'You must always bear in mind that it is you the Seigneur asked in marriage. Had he loved Mademoiselle King, he could have proposed to her.'

'I think he loves her.' Annette was twisting a tassel on the cushion as she spoke.

'She wants you to feel that,' Madame Lascie told her. 'But I am sure it is not so. I have talked with him and I feel that the Seigneur has a feeling for you, my child, but he fears to frighten you. He has the English view, he thinks you are too young.' The kind old eyes were shrewd as Madame Lascie went on: 'That is not so, is it, my little one? You are not too young?'

Recognizing the significance in the older woman's voice, Annette met her eyes steadily, bravely. 'No, Madame Lascie, I am not too young.'

Before Annette left, it was arranged that her riding lessons should be taken at Madame Lascie's house. Annette did not want Valda to know about them; she might insist on accompanying her—and that—that would not be tolerable!

Madame Lascie smiled. 'Whatever transpires, my child, you must go ahead. Ignore her, forget that she is there.'

Oh, it was easy to talk, Annette thought ruefully as later that day she sat in the lovely drawing-room while Valda spoke to Henry and his another sat in a chair, a book open on her lap, her eyes fixed thoughtfully on Annette's face.

'You don't play bridge?' Valda said, horrified when Annette had confessed she had never played. 'But all—' she paused, shrugging her shoulders.

Annette lifted her chin bravely. 'I'm studying the game. In Durban I bought a book about it.'

She was dismayed by the laughter that followed her innocent remark.

Henry's voice was kind—the voice of an adult talking to a child. 'It's impossible to learn from a book, but if you want to learn, we will teach you. There are four of us.'

Annette stared at him in horror. Did he want to make her look a fool? Was he on Valda's side? But what could she do?

Valda delightedly seized on the idea and immediately rang the bell for Rennie to come and prepare the table. And so started a new routine. Every night after dinner, Annette received a lesson in the art of playing bridge. Sometimes she wondered how she managed to sit through the ordeal with three faces watching her, three voices criticizing, blaming or instructing her, three pairs of eyes showing shocked surprise when she did something silly.

The lovely graceful room with its faded brocades and swinging chandelier lost all its charm for Annette as she struggled to remember all the things she found so easy to forget. How could she remember such things as conventions, what the method was, or how many cards had been played, and if the ace of spades was still there, when Henry's hand brushed hers lightly as he, as dummy, advised her what card to play. She had always thought card games were supposed to be fun, but this was a nightmare. Not even the hours she spent sitting up in bed at night studying the despised book on bridge helped her much.

Everything was so different. Valda had offered in front of Henry to teach Annette to play golf—and those lessons were a nightmare too. Everything was like a nightmare, the most ordinary thing distorted because of her fear of Valda.

And came one of those days when it seemed like the end. After breakfast, Henry had asked Annette to go to his study with him. She had felt rather than seen the triumphant look on Valda's face, so she was not too surprised when Henry said abruptly:

'Look, Annette, I'm sure you didn't mean to sound rude, but Valda told me the other day that—'

'Henri,' Annette said, her voice cold and altering under his thoughtful gaze, 'you mean—you refer to Marie? She did nothing that was wrong, except to put Valda's shoes in the wrong dace. It was not Marie's task to clean the shoes. She's not the shoe cleaner, nor is she Valda's maid.' Annette could speak more firmly now. Madame Lascie had groomed her well on the duties of the enormous staff the Chateau employed.

'Valda was trying to help you,' he began. 'After all, we can't have a different girl for every job.' His fingers drummed impatiently on the desk.

'Henri,' her voice trembled as she looked up at him. 'You always have done, so Madame Lascie explained it to me. It's not expensive to have so many servants as they have no great wants, they are content with a small salary and they work well.' Her eyes flashed. 'Now there is discord. Marie is in tears, and Rennie, who is—you may have forgotten—her mother's husband's aunt's niece.' She laughed, suddenly very near tears. 'Rennie is disturbed. He's afraid to trouble you, but—'

Henry's attention was caught. 'Say that again—her mother's husband's—surely you mean her father.'

Annette's dimples appeared unexpectedly. 'I thought that at first. It seems he is her mother's second husband.'

'I see. Then you say aunt's *niece—but* Rennie is a man,' Henry pointed out.

Annette's face dissolved in laughter. 'Yes, meant nephew. I get so confused with all these relationships. Do you realize that for years, ever since this Chateau was built, the servants have all been related? That's why you never lack staff.'

'And require so many,' he said dryly. He looked it her momentarily happy face and seemed to make a decision. 'Look, Annette, it's your place to handle the staff. You are to be the mistress here. Speaking French so fluently, you can sort out the muddles. I'll tell Valda. She means well but—'

Annette clasped her hands excitedly. 'Oh, Henri *merci*. Then Marie can stay?' He nodded and like a child she clapped her hands. 'Oh, goody, now there will be rejoicing.' She smiled at him and ran from the room, glad to be able to tell Rennie that the Seigneur had said there was a misunderstanding, that Marie need not go. What a difference it would make. The work had been done sullenly for the last few days, so differently from the Creoles' usual happy-go-lucky way of working.

Not that Henry's mother helped much. As Annette was going to Rennie, Mrs. Revoir called her. She was in the dining-room, running a critical finger along the polished heavy sideboard.

'Dust everywhere, Annette. If you're supposed to be learning to handle the staff, you're not succeeding very well,' she said, her voice cold.

'I'll speak about it,' Annette promised, hurrying away, knowing it was useless to point out that as the days grew hotter these unexpected spirals of wind that suddenly blew

125

up, whirling sand everywhere, meant you could dust the rooms a hundred times a day and still find sand in every room.

Of course Henry's mother did not like her. She strongly disapproved of the marriage and made no bones about it. She had said firmly that there must be an engagement of at least six months.

Annette smiled, pausing for a moment before going into Rennie's pantry, remembering Henry's reaction. He had looked up from packing his pipe and had smiled at his mother and had suggested three months.

'No, no,' she said at once. 'It's not long enough to get to know one another.'

'My dear *maman*,' Henry had said, deliberately teasing his mother, as Annette well knew, for Mrs. Revoir loathed to be reminded that there was French blood in her son. 'We can get know one another after we're married. We shall have all the time in the world, shan't we, Annette?' he had asked, smiling at his wife-to-be kindly.

Annette's heart had thumped so loudly that she felt all must hear it.

'Yes, all the time in the world,' she had said unsteadily.

Valda had laughed. 'It sounds like a like a sentence,' she mocked.

For once, Annette had found courage 'A lovely sentence, that's what it is,' she had said coolly, and felt absurdly elated because of the

126

fury in Valda's eyes.

As she was remembering this and thinking of Henry's decision to leave his bride-to-be in charge of the staff, Annette allowed herself to hope a little. If he meant to break off the engagement, to marry Valda, surely he would not put Annette in charge of the staff!

Rennie leapt to his feet as she pushed open the swing door of the pantry. He had been sitting in a rocking chair, reading a very old newspaper. *'Messie?'* he asked worriedly. He must have heard Henry ask her to go to the study.

Impulsively she put her hand on his. 'Rennie, all is well.' Automatically she talked in French. Rennie spoke and understood English, after a fashion, but he was most at ease in French. 'The Seigneur says there has been a misunderstanding and that Marie must stay with us—if she will,' Annette added, knowing the secret pride this family that had served the Revoirs so long and so faithfully possessed.

Rennie was on one knee, kissing her hand. Words tumbled out of his mouth. Tales of their fears of what could happen to Marie, far from his watchful eye; that she would marry well from the Chateau, that if she left everyone would talk about the reason for it. 'The Revoirs,' he finished proudly, 'have never dismissed one of us.'

They dismissed themselves, Madame Lascie

had explained to Annette. Their position at the Chateau was one they were proud of, so that if any member of their family misbehaved, his own relations would force him to resign.

Later, Annette was in the small room, the annexe to the drawing-room, sitting before the aged spinet, tentatively trying to play, loving the sweet tinkling notes, when Valda came into the room. Hastily Annette stood up, turning her back on the spinet, closing the lid, and dreading Valda's sarcasm.

But Valda was engrossed. She had a notebook and pencil in her hand as she looked round her. 'This room,' she said thoughtfully. 'I think if that wall was knocked down and—'

'But we don't want it knocked down,' Annette said. She loved the quiet cool little room, loved it as she did the strange three-cornered room that Madame Lascie had used as her private sitting-room.

'You may not,' Valda said, her voice amused 'but Henry will, when I've spoken to him. This whole place needs repairing and renovating. It's in a shocking state.'

She walked out of the room before Annette could answer her. Annette stood, clinging to the spinet for support. Surely Henry would not listen to Valda? He might—if Valda suggested that the Islanders would think he was mean if he did not. Had Valda discovered that Achilles' heel of Henry's? Annette wondered anxiously. She had her own plans for the

Chateau and one day she would find courage enough to suggest them to him.

CHAPTER NINE

Hating the atmosphere in the Chateau, Annette went through the scorching heat down the hill to the Cascas' house. Everything looked shrivelled and brown, the rains were late, everywhere yearned for water. She saw that her father's house had been painted, that small crisp white net curtains were at the windows. She wondered who was living there. She must ask Henry.

The shrill screaming noise the parakeets made as they came swooping out of the trees assailed her ears. She stood to watch the green shining birds as they flashed past.

Madame Casca was alone, delighted to see Annette.

'It is so long, my child, since you visited us Why is this? Have Madame Revoir and Mademoiselle King made you also a snob?' she asked.

Annette laughed, curling up in the wicker chair looking lovingly at the great ocean breakers as: they raced in roaring loudly, sending spray high in the air. 'It's difficult to get away, what with golf lessons and bridge,' she exclaimed.

She made Madame Casca laugh with her descriptions of the bridge lessons. 'I shall never learn,' Annette finished, her voice discouraged. 'Valda has that effect on me. She will always win.'

Madame Casca's face showed signs of agitation. 'You must fight her,' she said fiercely. 'Do not be soft. She knows no mercy, and you should not show any either.'

'But I don't want to have to fight,' Annette said.

Madame Casca threw up her hands in horror. '*Nom de dieu*, what woman does not have to fight for her man? You must do the same.'

As Annette walked home, the sun was low, the distant mountains fading from olive to a beautiful lilac, and then as the sun clipped out of sight the sky was a wonderful pale gold, rose and turquoise.

Henry, his mother and Valda were sitting on the terrace, cool drinks at their elbows. They watched Annette as she walked up the shallow steps and hesitated, looking at them.

'Visiting?' Valda asked, her voice friendly. That, of course, was for Henry's benefit, Annette thought miserably, her happy afternoon behind her.

'The Cascas,' she told them.

Valda looked amused. 'Don't tell me that wastrel Jean is still living on his mother and the Revoirs?' she asked.

Annette felt her cheeks grow hot; she opened her mouth, quick to leap to the defence of her friends. Then she closed it. It was true. Her father had said so and she had seen it for herself.

'He's amusing,' she said quietly, murmuring an excuse about a bath and changing her frock.

'I suppose he is, for a child like you,' Valda said in a tolerant voice.

Henry stood up. 'Would you like a cool drink, Annette?' he asked.

She looked up at him and her heart seemed to turn over. She loved him so much—every inch of this big, impressive-looking man, with the dark red hair and the stern mouth, the kindness and the unpredictable bursts of anger. Suddenly she understood what Madame Casca had meant; suddenly she wanted to fight, tooth and nail for Henry. And then she remembered Madame Casca's anxious words as they parted: 'Do not worry, my little one,' she had said. 'The worst thing you can do is to show dismay. The Seigneur is not the kind of man to break his word,' she had said.

But Annette did not want Henry to marry her simply because he 'did not break his word'.

Now she smiled. 'No, thank you, Henri darling,' she said lightly. 'It was too hot down there and I long for a bath.'

He nodded, looking at her in a strange way 'Later, then.'

She went indoors, conscious that he was

131

staring at her, wondering why he looked so odd.

Annette managed to prolong her bath so that she went downstairs to dinner with just a short time to spare for an iced drink. She sat quietly in a corner of the high-backed couch, listening to an animated discussion between Valda and Henry. Every now and then his mother glanced at Annette and then at the other couple with a significant look. Annette listened vaguely. They were talking about people she had never heard of, discussing something she did not know existed. Valda and Henry had lived in a different world from hers; they were bound together by ties that could never be broken. Looking at the vivacious Valda, her eyes sparkling, her lovely figure displayed to advantage in the truly elegant black frock, Annette wondered how Henry could bear not to take the lovely creature in his arms.

Perhaps he did.

The thought spoiled her dinner, made her quiet and unable to respond to Valda's teasing. It was even worse then, when they began to play bridge. Annette could not concentrate. Would Henry giver tell her that he regretted his decision? That he wanted to marry Valda?

She struggled to remember all she had been taught as she listened to the other bids, and made her own. She thought Valda looked amused, but her mind was too confused, too worried about her new fears, to care.

Her brow furrowed anxiously as she gazed blankly at the cards in her hand. Suddenly they didn't mean a thing. She tried to remember what had been bid, she hoped for the best as she threw a card on the table.

'Really, Annette,' Valda, her partner, said with a light laugh. 'Do concentrate, my dear child.'

Funny, when Valda called her that, it was an insult; but if Madame Lascie, or even Henry called her it, she did not mind.

'We're waiting, Annette,' Henry's mother said impatiently.

With a feeling of joy, Annette saw the ace in her hand. She threw it down. That would show them that she had profited by their patience.

There was an appalled hush. Annette looked at Henry's amazed face, at Valda's exaggerated dismay, at Mrs. Revoir's irritation.

'Shouldn't I have played it?' Annette asked, her voice trembling.

Valda threw her cards down. 'I give up,' she said, and began to laugh. 'You can't help it, Annette; you're too young and innocent.'

Annette's cheeks flamed as Valda's teasing barb struck home. She instinctively turned to Henry.

'I'm sorry, Henri,' she said in distress.

He laughed gently. 'It's no tragedy, my dear child. Anyhow, it's too hot to play. What about some music, Valda?'

Valda stood up, stretching like a graceful lazy tiger. 'I can't play on that awful spinet you have, but—' her mouth curved into a smile, 'Annette can. I heard her this morning.'

'Annette?' Henry turned to the girl by his side with surprise. 'I didn't know you played. We must get the spinet repaired, if it needs it. Will you play for us?'

Annette twisted her hands miserably. She hated Valda more in that moment than before. Valda must have heard Annette's pathetic attempts that morning and wanted to make her look a fool.

She lifted her head and managed a smile. 'I'm terribly out of practice, but I used to teach music at my aunt's school—or rather help the girls with their practice,' she added. And how she had hated it! Listening to scales played a hundred times over, played reluctantly, rebelliously, angrily. 'If I leave the two doors open you can hear it in here.'

Valda had gone to sit on the couch. 'And how we will suffer,' she said softly, but not too softly for Annette to hear as she passed on the way to the door.

Annette sat before the spinet, gazing at the faded golden-brown satinwood, wondering how many women had sat before it, their hands trembling, their hearts full of love, praying, as she was, that she might not make a fool of herself. In the morning she had been trying to play some works of Chopin that she

134

had always found difficult. Now she would be less ambitious.

Her fingers wandered over the old faded keys, finding little tunes travelling from her mind to her fingers. Soft, tinkling music that spoke of days long past, of bewigged ladies and portly gentlemen, of balls, and lovers holding hands behind the palm trees in the small conservatory, of whispered words of love.

She was shocked when she heard the silvery chimes of the little French travelling clock on the small table in the corner. Had she played so long? They must have gone to bed long ago.

As she closed the spinet, Henry came into the room. He was yawning.

'Thank you, Annette, I enjoyed that very much,' he said.

She jumped to her feet, turning to look at him with wide dismayed eyes.

'I'm sorry I played for so long,' she said breathlessly. 'I—I just forgot the time.'

Henry stood there, staring at her; his dark trousers, white jacket and red cummerbund suiting him to perfection.

'Don't apologize, Annette,' he said, a quizzical smile on his mouth.

Her face burned with confusion. 'But . . . but you must have been terribly bored.'

He frowned. 'Look, I've just told you that I enjoyed it very much. Either I'm a liar or—'

She wanted to run away. Why must everything she said to this man get twisted? 'I

135

didn't mean that. It's just that I don't play very well, and—'

Suddenly his hands were on her shoulders, hands whose warm strength burned through the thin cream silk of her frock.

'Annette,' he said, and his voice was sharp with displeasure. 'Please stop this childish habit of apologizing for everything you do. You play extremely well and with great feeling. It seemed to me that at last you were growing up. Your music was that of an adult woman— yet now you are a child again.'

She blinked rapidly, terrified lest he see the tears in her eyes.

'I am an adult,' she said, her voice trembling a little.

'Then act like one,' he told her.

'I—I—' she began, and stopped, for she was conscious in every nerve of her body of his warm hands still on her shoulders; of his nearness, his dearness.

'What were you thinking about as you played?' he demanded.

Again her cheeks were hot. She could not tell him the truth—that she had been dreaming of the days when they would be alone together. She tried to look away, but his gold-flecked green eyes seemed to exert some magnetic force as she looked into them. 'I was thinking of all the women who had played on that spinet,' she said—and in a way it was the truth. 'And—and wondering about them. If

136

they were happy or sad, if the men they loved cared for another—'

'Grave thoughts,' he said, and a little smile played round his stern mouth. 'I thought girls of your age only dreamed of themselves and their futures. I didn't think they had time to think about other people.'

Was he teasing her? If only she could tell. She was never sure when to laugh or be serious. With Henry, it was always so difficult.

'The Chateau makes you think about others,' she said soberly.

He lifted one thick eyebrow as if in question. 'I believe you really like the Chateau.'

'I love it,' she said earnestly.

Dare she speak to him of Valda's plans to pull down walls and make alterations? It worried her so much, for often she found Valda with her notebook, eyeing a cupboard, measuring an alcove.

She was startled when, with a swift movement, he pulled her towards him so that as he looked down at her she could see herself reflected in his eyes. She began to tremble.

'Are you growing up at last, Annette?' he asked suddenly. 'Or are you still afraid of me?'

The stillness seemed to enfold them. There was not a sound in the great house, not even the creak of old wood or the squeak of a mouse; not even the hoot of an owl from outside, the chirrup of a cicada, or the bark of a dog.

They were completely alone. It was as if no one else in the world existed

'I'm—I'm not afraid of you, Henri,' she told him softly. 'Only—only when you're cross with me.'

He frowned at that. 'But I'm never cross with you.' As he spoke, he let his hands fall from her shoulders and moved away. He looked distressed.

She shivered. What had happened to that wonderful moment when they had been so close? How had she destroyed it?

She managed a light laugh. It tinkled mockingly in the quiet room like a silver bell. 'Oh, Henri!' she said, and tried to smile 'But you're often cross with me.' His grave gaze confused her still more, so she went on, doing her best to lighten the tension that was suddenly in the air. 'Then you talk with a loud voice and I tremble.

Her hands were clenched as she fought the bitter disappointment that filled her. She had been so sure he was going to kiss her. And then everything would have been all right. If only he would kiss her—then she could put all her love into that kiss and he would surely know.

He was staring at her with a puzzled frown—this tall handsome man with the red hair and strange eyes, this man with the controlled face and the stern mouth, this man

138

who could be so kind and—and yet so cruel.

'You *are* afraid of me,' he said slowly.

She bit her lip nervously. 'Only of your displeasure, Henri.'

'You never displease me,' he told her.

Again she took refuge in brittle laughter. 'What about my attempts to play bridge?' she asked. There was a little silence, and then she sighed and forgot to try to sound gay. 'I tried so hard, Henri,' she said very quietly, 'But it was no good.'

Although they were still standing close together now it seemed as if a hundred miles separated them as he looked at her with cold, critical eyes.

'As I said before,' he began, his voice suddenly harsh, 'you will belittle yourself. You're your own worst enemy. You've made up your mind you will never be able to play bridge and so you can't! Valda says it's the same with golf. You have no confidence in yourself whatsoever. It's quite absurd,' he went on, his voice, perhaps unconsciously, rising. 'At your age, you shoulc be on top of the world—able to do anything, afraid of no one.'

'Oh, but you're wrong; quite, quite wrong, Henri,' she said, the strength of her conviction giving her the courage to disagree. 'At my age one is terribly unsure. One needs encouragement praise, appreciation.'

'Well, I do appreciate you.' Was there a reproachful note in his voice? 'Didn't I say I

139

enjoyed your playing?'

She looked at him sadly. 'But, Henri, I think that perhaps you were just being polite—or—or kind.'

With startling force, his hands gripped her shoulders and he shook her violently. When he let her go—just as abruptly—the world seemed to spin and she put out her hands blindly and clung to him for a moment.

'Look,' he said harshly, 'I told you I enjoyed your music, and I don't tell lies.'

She let go of him as the world steadied, and stared up at him, bewildered at the way his anger had flared up.

'Please get into your silly little head,' he went on, 'the fact that I don't tell lies—either to be polite or kind. Now go to bed and get some beauty sleep.' He turned away from her, speaking gruffly over his shoulder: 'Good night.'

'Good night, Henri,' she gasped, and slipped away to the sanctuary of her room.

As she undressed swiftly, she stared out of the window at the beautiful, eerie, moonlit world. If only Henry wasn't so unpredictable. If only it wasn't so terribly easy to say just one little wrong word and make his whole mood change. He had told her not to belittle herself. Had he any idea how difficult it was to learn anything from a person like Valda, who destroyed what little confidence you had?

Valda. It was always Valda who came

between them. Valda who made critical remarks, who spoiled everything. If only she knew if he was in love with Valda.

Madame Lascie had pointed out that Henry had not proposed marriage to Valda but to Annette.

Madame Casca had said that she must fight for Henry. That all women fought for the men they loved.

But Madame Casca had also said there was no need to worry—that Henry Revoir was not the type of man to break his word!

Annette shivered, despite the warmth of the tropical night. There lay the prick—the thorn that never left her. She did not want Henry to marry her simply because he was a man who could not break his word. What sort of marriage could they build together if all the time he was thinking about Valda? If he always regretted the promise he had given to Annette's father?

It took her a long time to go to sleep and she awoke later than usual. Fearing a sarcastic comment, she hurried along the corridor, and as she passed the half-open door of the room belonging to Mrs. Revoir, it was impossible to avoid hearing the clear, acid-tinged voice say, 'Really, Valda, you do appear to be slipping. You told me you could persuade Henry to sell the Island and return to London, but it seems that he still intends to marry that insipid child.'

Annette sped by the door and down the

stairs, her cheeks burning. Was she *insipid?* Was that what Henry had meant when he scolded her?

With shaking hands, she helped herself to kidneys and bacon and sausages.

'I thought you disliked sausages,' Henry said suddenly, his voice amused.

Annette jumped. He must have followed her into the room. She lifted dismayed eyes and saw that he was smiling.

'I wasn't thinking,' she confessed, and put the sausages back into the silver warming-dish.

'Dreaming—as usual?' Valda asked in a cool contemptuous voice as she entered the room and came to stand near them at the enormous walnut sideboard, and helped herself. 'Did you have to force yourself to stay awake last night, my poor Henry?' she asked lightly as they seated themselves.

Annette did not hear his reply for she was trying to force food that tasted of sawdust down her throat. *Insipid . . .* Was she insipid? A dreamer? It seemed as if nothing she ever did was right. Belittling herself. Acting like a child. Her eyes stung, so she kept them fixed on her plate, afraid lest Valda might see.

'And what took possession of you last night, Annette?' Valda asked, her voice amused. 'You were like the babbling brook—we thought you were never going to stop playing.'

Annette's cheeks burned. She looked up, an apologetic answer ready on her lips.

142

Then she saw that Henry was looking at her with a significant smile, so she lifted her chin defiantly and made her voice gay.

'I'm afraid I was enjoying myself so much, Valda,' she said lightly, 'that I completely forgot the time.'

'And so did I,' Henry joined in, his grave voice approving. 'It was a pleasant evening, and I'm hoping to persuade Annette to often repeat it, for I found it most relaxing.'

'What a very polite way of saying you were bored,' Valda commented, her eyes amused. 'But then you are always so gallant, Henry.'

Henry smiled. 'I'm afraid Annette doesn't think so,' he said, and began to laugh. 'She says that I talk with a loud voice. Isn't that so, Annette?' he asked.

Annette thought her cheeks would never feel cool again. How could he! She looked at him reproachfully. His eyes were twinkling, and she realized, with a shock, that he was actually baiting Valda!

'You're quite right, Henri,' Annette said meekly, trying to look demure, fluttering her lashes a little, glancing at him quickly. 'You often make a great noise about very little.'

'Really!' Valda cried, shocked. 'How dare you be so rude?' She turned to Henry. 'What do you—'

But he was chuckling as he rolled his napkin and slid it into its silver ring. 'It isn't rude, for it happens to be the truth.' He gave Annette

143

an approving, encouraging smile. 'While we're being so frank, Annette, tell me some more of my failings,' he asked, his voice teasing.

She stared at him in some dismay and then found courage.

'Well,' she said very slowly. 'I think you're the kindest man I know—but you're always afraid that people will think your kindness is a sign of weakness.'

'Touché,' he said, and sounded pleased. 'And what is your weakness, Annette?'

She was terrified lest she say the wrong thing and his mood change.

'I—I accept other people's opinion of me.'

He laughed outright. 'How right you are. You lack confidence in yourself. Now what about Valda?'

Annette turned to look at the beautiful girl, who was a dazzling sight in her white frock with her flaming red hair piled high on her head and an arrogant look on her face.

'Valda?' Annette asked. 'I don't think Valda has a weakness, for she is clever as well as beautiful. I wish she would teach me,' Annette went on, and meant it sincerely. 'I know she doesn't suffer fools gladly, but I'm sure a young girl can learn a lot from a mature woman,' she added wistfully.

'I wonder if you could,' Henry said in a queer strangled voice as he rose. To Annette's amazement she saw that he was trying not to laugh. Why? What had she said that was amusing? And why was Valda glaring at her like that?

Hadn't he told her to have more confidence it herself? Hadn't he encouraged her to go on?

Maybe he meant in other ways, too. Maybe she should act like an engaged girl instead of always treating him so formally. Perhaps he would like it if she showed sometimes how much she liked him. *Like?* What a neutral sort of wishy-washy word to describe what she felt for Henry.

She went to his side, tucking her hand through his arm. 'I'll see you off, Henri,' she said.

The palms of her hands were sticky with nervousness, but she held her head high as she went out with Henry to the car, very conscious of Valda's furious eyes boring into her back.

As Henry settled himself behind the steering wheel and the sun glinted on his red hair, his eyes were twinkling as he smiled at her, 'You're learning fast, Annette,' he said.

'Too fast?' she asked, suddenly afraid.

'It couldn't be too fast,' he told her, and with that cryptic remark drove away.

She stood in the sunshine for a long time, gazing after the car wistfully. If only one day he would ask her to go with him!

CHAPTER TEN

Life at the Chateau was only bearable when Henry was at home, so Annette seized every chance to slip away quietly. Loving the Island as she did, she was always happy exploring it, sometimes on the black horse Henry had bought her. Sometimes she would drive the car along the narrow twisting roads. She had many friends and made many new ones. One of these was the Mother Superior at the convent, and Annette always felt better for having seen the elderly nun with the serene face and the gentle smile.

One day as Annette was admiring the exquisite embroidery, the beautiful handmade lace and the sewing done by the pupils, she had a wonderful idea.

'Would you make my wedding-dress?' she asked.

She was startled by the response. The quiet convent seemed to leap to life as designs were produced, samples of beautiful lace examined. The pale waxen skin on the Mother Superior's face was flushed and her eyes shone as she thanked Annette warmly, and said that it was a great honour, a wonderful encouragement, and, riding home through the heat, Annette thought humbly how wonderful it was to be able to give so much pleasure in such an effortless way.

Another friend she frequently visited was Father Leonardo Severini, a middle-aged Italian priest, it the mission which sprawled on the hills above the blue lagoon. He was an old friend of her father's and she loved to sit listening to him, her heart warming, feeling that her father was not so far away after all. Often, too, they discussed Henry Revoir and his troubles and Annette knew that Henry had a real friend in Father Leonardo, a friend he might one day need. Father Leonardo had been sympathetic, too, when Annette told him of her fears, of Valda's domination, her plans to rebuild the Chateau.

'But you must fight this woman,' he said firmly. 'It is you the Seigneur proposes to marry—the Chateau will be your home.'

So one evening Annette gathered her courage and seized a moment when, after an excellent dinner, they were talking in the drawing-room, the screened windows wide open to the beautiful ropical night, the great yellow moon in the star-spangled sky, the cicadas shrilling in the background. Henry was laughing a lot and seemed in a good mood, so she went to sit by him and finally caught his attention.

'Henri—' Annette began, in her eager nervous little voice, brushing back the fringe that felt so hot on such a night, 'Valda has been kind enough to offer advice about the

Chateau, but I feel we have no occasion to hurry ourselves. I don't feel we should pull down walls.'

Valda sat up with a jerk, her cheeks red, her eyes angry. 'I said nothing about pulling down walls!' she declared.

Annette looked at her. Father Leonardo had said this must be handled carefully. 'Then I must have made a mistake, Valda,' she said meekly. 'And for that I apologize.' Father Leonardo had said that the gentle answer turneth away wrath. She looked quickly at the silent man by her side. 'Henri—it seems I'm wrong, but it was the day I was practising on the spinet, and Valda came in and said the wall should be knocked down and the little room become part of the drawing-room. I said that I didn't think you would wish it, Henri—' Her eyes were wide and distressed because of the silence in the room. 'But she said you would agree with her.'

'There appears to be a general misunderstanding,' Henry said coldly. 'I understood from Valda that *you* wanted to rebuild the Chateau and that she was trying to restrain you.'

'Rebuild it?' Annette cried in horror. 'But to rebuild it would be to destroy its character.'

He smiled at her. 'That's exactly how I feel,' he said. He turned to look across the room at the furious Valda. 'Thank you, Valda,' he said very politely, 'but as this is to be our home, I think can leave it to us to decide what should

148

be done.'

Valda's eyes were blazing, her voice trembled. 'I only want to help,' she protested.

'We appreciate that,' he said dryly. He leaned forward and took one of Annette's hands in his. 'Don't we, Annette?' he asked, smiling down at her.

'Of course we do. Very much,' Annette said, confused; very conscious of his hand on hers, startled that she had beaten Valda so easily, sorry for the discomfited girl, wishing that Mrs. Revoir was not looking so maliciously pleased.

Henry pulled her to her feet suddenly. 'Come and play for me, Annette,' he said, and his voice was, for once, gentle.

At the spinet, she let herself dream for a moment. She had fought Valda over one thing—and won. Did that mean that she could always win? Was it her own fault for not trying? Was that why Henry always saw her as a child?

But the little victory was a hollow one, and a few days later she rode home from the convent on an oppressively hot day, trying not to feel depressed. It seemed as if for every step forward she took with Henry, she slipped back two steps, thanks to Valda's hints, gibes, and habit of talking to Henry about people and things of which Annette knew nothing, always emphasizing her youth.

Annette had a bath and washed her dusty hair, and then lay on the chaise-longue before the open window, closing her eyes wearily.

The door opened and Annette looked up. It was Henry's mother. Hastily she got up, very conscious of the loose dressing-gown, her bare feet, her wet hair, as she stared in dismay at Mrs. Revoir, cold and glittering in a tomato red sheath frock, diamonds in her ears and on her fingers.

'I must talk to you,' Henry's mother said firmly and coldly. 'This farce must end. I don't blame you for wanting security. I blame my son for promising your father to marry you. It is most unsuitable marriage. Valda is the ideal wife for Henry. He must get rid of the Island and—'

Annette was staring unhappily at the angry woman. 'And me?' she said.

Her quietness seemed to stop Mrs. Revoir, for the anger left her. She stared at Annette thoughtfully. 'I will give you ten thousand pounds,' she said, 'if you will break off the engagement and leave the Island.'

Annette caught her breath. Did Mrs. Revoi think she could be bought? Did they all believ she was marrying Henry for his money?

She closed her eyes, fighting the desire to say cruel, unforgettable things; the longing to rus to Henry and tell him of the terrible insult.

Somehow she made herself speak. 'I'm sorry Mrs. Revoir, but I'm going to marry Henri, she said firmly. She looked at the startled angry face and found compassion for it. Maybe

Henry's mother thought she was doing it for the best. 'I will do my best to make him happy,' Annette said simply.

Mrs. Revoir stared at her, the colour leaving her flushed cheeks. She opened her mouth and closed it again and then, without another word, left the room.

Alone, Annette wept a little; wept for the ugliness of the scene, the humiliation. Could no one see that she loved Henry? She gazed out of the window at the deep blue of the sea and remembered the cruel words. Was it true, then, that Henry *had* promised her father to marry her? Was that what Madame Casca had meant when she said Henry was not a man to break his word?

Suddenly she was trembling, her hands shaking. She had to know the truth. If he loved Valda still—if he was keeping a death-bed promise—

She bathed her eyes in cold water and carefully made up. It was Friday, so he would be in his office.

She found him, bent over ledgers. He looked up, frowning a little as if not pleased with the interruption. And then he came to her, made her sit down and asked in a concerned voice what was wrong.

His kindness was nearly her undoing for she had to screw up her eyes tightly to keep the tears back. Her new-found courage began to evaporate. She looked at this big strong

151

man she loved so much—her eyes found the little mole she longed to touch. Had she to say goodbye to him—to put all hope of winning his love behind her?

Yet she must know. She could not go on any longer, fearing, wondering.

'Henri,' she said softly, clenching her fists tightly in her lap, 'did you promise my father to marry me?'

He looked startled. 'I did not—' he said sharply as he sat down and lighted a cigarette. He looked at her. 'Why?'

She stared in the greeny-gold eyes and saw that he told the truth.

'But everyone says—' she began.

He frowned. 'I promised your father I would look after you. That didn't necessarily mean marriage.'

She swallowed nervously. 'Then—then you do want to marry me?' she asked him, quickly crossing her fingers, praying that the answer would be *Yes*.

But Henry never gave a simple answer. 'Would I have asked you to marry me unless I wanted you to do so?' he asked in turn.

She sighed as they stared at one another. And suddenly she was frightened. Why was he so quiet? Was anger boiling up inside him? Had she offended him? 'I'm sorry, Henri,' she said quickly. 'I didn't mean to vex you, but— but I wouldn't want you to marry me if you didn't want to.'

152

'My dear child,' he said, and the exasperation in his voice alarmed her still more. 'I'm old enough to know my own mind. No one could force me into a marriage I didn't desire.' He began to speak more rapidly and she shrank back in her chair as she listened, staring wide-eyed at him. 'Have I to go on my bended knees every day of my life and ask you to marry me, with my hand on my heart?' He demonstrated with one hand, and as if the movement had made him see the humour of the situation, he began to laugh. Then he said gently, 'Is that what you want?'

She relaxed a little. 'Of course not, Henri it's just—'

'Just that you don't want me to marry you if don't want to,' he said the words for her, still smiling. 'Very sensible of you, Annette.'

She stared at the copper-red hair, the strong face, the sweet little mole, and her heart seemed to turn over. He wanted to marry her.

He went on, and her heart sank again. 'We share the same interests, Annette. We both love the Island. I'm sure we can make a success of our marriage,' he said quietly. She stared at him miserably. So he was going to marry her because she could be useful to him. What a fool she was—why did she go on hoping? Henry was not a romantic man. This was to be a sensible marriage with no nonsense about love. She sighed, staring unhappily at her hands. All the same, was not a sensible

153

marriage better than no marriage at all? She looked up at him swiftly before she lost courage.

'Henri—would you—could we—' she began and took a deep breath. 'Could we be married soon?' The words came out in a rush.

'Immediately?' he asked in a surprised voice and she thought she also heard dismay in it.

She swallowed and nodded. 'As soon as possible.' She hoped he would not ask for her reasons. If he did, what could she say? She could not tell the truth—that she was afraid of his mother and of Valda.

He leaned forward and gazed at her. 'Are you sure you want to marry me?' he asked.

Her heart thumped wildly, but she looked frankly into his eyes. 'Quite sure,' she said quietly.

He stood up abruptly, thrusting his hands into his pockets, looking down at her. 'Very well,' he said. He waited until she was standing and then added casually, 'I'll make the necessary arrangements.' He waited until she had her hand on the door-knob and then said, 'What about your wedding-dress?'

She turned. 'I've—I've arranged with the Mother Superior. The sisters are going to make it,' she added a little nervously.

He merely appeared amused as he said, 'Oh, you have, have you?' As she left the room, she wondered what he could find funny in that.

It was only when she was outside the door, trembling with relief because the ordeal was over, that she remembered that she had forgotten to ask the most important question of all: was he still in love with Valda?

She dared not go back and interrupt him again. A little sadly she went up to her room. At least they were to be married soon!

CHAPTER ELEVEN

At dinner the next day, Henry said casually 'By the way, Mother, I want you to help me draw up a list of guests. We're being married in a month's time.'

There was a little silence as the two footmen collected the plates and Rennie moved majestically at one end of the room.

'You're just like your father,' Mrs. Revoir said with a sigh. 'Just as stubborn and as big a fool.'

Henry's eyes twinkled. 'I trust Annette doesn't think so,' he said with a smile for the quiet girl who sat so very still.

Annette smiled back at him gratefully. 'Would I marry you if I thought you a fool?' she asked lightly.

'A month?' Valda said as if she had just found her tongue. Her fingers tore at the roll

155

on her plate. 'That's not enough time, Henry. Her wedding-dress—'

'Everything is under control,' Henry said cheerfully. 'The sisters at the convent are making it.'

Valda stared at him 'Are you mad? The convent!' Her voice was scornful.

'They make the most beautiful lace,' Annette said very quickly, terrified because for a moment there was an uncertain look on Henry's face. They could not change their minds now. What would the Mother Superior feel like? It would be an insult.

Unexpectedly Mrs. Revoir came to the rescue. 'If it's a rag, it's Annette's own fault,' she said. 'There's no time to make other arrangements.'

Relaxing, Annette listened in silence as Mrs. Revoir and Henry discussed plans. Valda also sat silently, but every now and then, if Annette looked at her, she found that Valda was staring at her with a strangely malignant expression. It made Annette feel uncomfortable, a little nervous. Which was absurd, for once she and Henry were married, there would be nothing to fear. All the same, it was a relief when the meal came to an end and, pleading a headache, Annette could slip away to her room.

In the days that followed, Mrs. Revoir plunged into the preparations for the wedding. Valda said very little, merely staring at

Annette all the time and making her wonder uneasily what Valda could be planning, as she sat with that sulky droop to her mouth, her eyes so thoughtful. Annette kept out of the way as much as possible, and on one hot day she rode back from the mission, her head aching, thinking guiltily that she had forgotten to take either hat or sunshade with her. She rode slowly, not very eager to get home, for she dreaded going back to such a strained atmosphere.

When the groom came for the horse and she went on to the terrace where the others were sitting, Henry looked up with a frown. 'You're very flushed,' he said, and got up. 'Don't tell me,' he went on in an exasperated voice, 'that you went out without a hat. How many times have I told you?'

Annette had no excuse as she looked up at him miserably, only that she had rushed out of the Chateau in a panic because Valda had said that some time they must talk together. Was Valda going to offer her twenty thousand pounds? There would surely be an ugly scene. But she could not tell Henry that.

He marched her into the cool house. 'Go straight to bed,' he ordered in a vexed voice. 'Take the tablets I send up to you.'

Once inside the house, he suddenly gripped her arm and looked down at her. 'I don't want to know where you spend all your time,' he said fiercely, 'for I am not your jailor, but—

but I must ask you to be a little more discreet, Annette.'

She stared up at him, startled by the sudden attack, not understanding it.

He frowned. 'You must know that people are talking about you and Jean Casca,' he said.

People? Why didn't he say outright that Valda was talking?

His grip tightened on her arm. 'Are you listening? How do you think I like having your name bandied about?'

Her heart seemed to sink as she looked at his angry face.

'I think,' she said in a small, weary voice, 'that you might trust me.'

'I do trust you,' he said angrily, letting go her arm. 'But I don't like people talking. How do you think I feel?'

She rubbed her arm which felt sore from his rough clutch. She looked up at his stern mouth and sighed.

'Sometimes I wonder if you *can* feel,' she said softly, and slipped away and up the stairs, seeing the startled look on his face, but not caring any more.

She felt suddenly tired of it all. Maybe it was her head that throbbed—maybe the oppressive heat of the day—maybe the long talk she had had with Father Leonardo—maybe the fact that Henry listened to others rather than to herself.

Maybe it was Henry himself. Could she

158

never do anything right? She was tired of trying to win his approval, tired of fighting Valda, tired of everything.

She had a quick bath and slid between the cool sheets with a grateful sigh. She swallowed the tablets and fell into a dreamless sleep.

In the morning, her head still ached and she felt desperately weary.

Henry came to see how she was and looked at her anxiously.

'I think you should see the doctor,' he said.

She felt too tired to argue with him and merely closed her eyes. It was a great weariness that possessed her, a feeling of hopelessness. Even though they were to be married, there was still Valda to fear.

The doctor, a plump, gallant little man, asked her a few questions, shook his head wisely as he saw how easily her eyes filled with tears.

'There is no need to worry, mademoiselle,' he said kindly. 'You need a rest.'

She heard him talking to Henry, his voice sharp with authority.

'Mademoiselle suffers from nerves— probably the result of delayed shock. I would advise that she stays in bed until she feels herself.'

It was easier to accept the verdict and lie there quietly, waited on by the little maid, visited twice a day by Henry, who continued to look at her anxiously. Oh, the bliss of being away from it all. How wonderful not to have to face Valda's constant scorn or Mrs. Revoir's quick critical glances—wonderful to have Henry so attentive and kind, not to have to fear his anger.

Sometimes, lying there blissfully, she would feel ashamed of herself, for she was shamming—yet, in a way, she was not, for she certainly did not feel herself. Here she was safe, contented, happy.

Now there was time to read her father's notes—to have him come to life again as she read about the Revoirs. She learned that it was a lie that had been spread wilfully round the Island—that Henry had not fought in the war. Here she had proof that he had—that he had even been decorated. She read of minerals that had been found on the Island. There was a surveyor's map and copious notes and then an explanation in her father's writing.

'*Le Colonel* told me to destroy these, but I kept them, for I feel that Henry should have the right to make a decision. His father feared that the Island might be exploited and the people suffer, but I feel if it is handled properly, the minerals could put the Island on a self-paying basis: Much better for all. Do not give this to Henry until you have got rid of Jacques Le Roy. He is not to be trusted.'

160

She folded the notes away and locked them up. Everyone seemed so sure that once she was married to Henry, she would have the power to get rid of the *avocat*. But would the mere act of marriage give her any more influence over Henry than she had now?

Propped comfortably against pillows, curtains drawn against the blinding sun, waited on, never harried or teased, or bullied or frightened, the days slipped by for Annette in a happy dream.

One day she awoke suddenly from an after-lunch siesta and looked round the darkened room and realized what she had done. She sat up, her heart filled with fear. She had handed Henry to Valda, as if on a silver platter.

What lies had Valda told him? What had she implied? What traps for Annette had she been able to lay?

How could she have been so stupid? Annette leapt from her bed and hurried to draw back the curtains. It was a strange, frightening world she looked on. Where had the sun gone? And the blue waters rippled by a breeze? There was no sunshine. The air seemed filled with a grey heavy dust. The lagoon was like turgid oil, the leaves of the palm trees drooped.

Feeling absurdly weak, she dressed. Outside her room it seemed as if the greyness of the outside world had penetrated the Chateau. It

161

hung about like an evil miasma rising from a marsh. The floors were dull, the windows dirty, the great silver vases were tarnished. As she went downstairs, she saw that the flowers in the hall were dead. Everywhere there was an air of neglect—almost of a house abandoned.

What could have happened? As she opened the door of the drawing-room, three faces turned to stare at her.

Annette clung to the door post, her knees suddenly like jelly. Why did they all look so tense, so angry? What could have happened?

Henry came hurriedly to her side. 'Should you be up?' he asked in a kind, concerned voice as he helped her to a chair.

She was glad to sink into it as she looked round in dismay at the beautiful room that had been so neglected. There was a dullness about the furniture—an air of decay. 'I'm all right,' she said a little impatiently. 'But what has happened?'

Mrs. Revoir, sitting in a straight-backed chair, tapping her hand restlessly on the arm of it, looked at her grimly, her eyes glittering. Valda stood before the windows, her cheeks red, her eyes flashing.

'Nothing much,' Henry drawled as he went to stand in front of the uncleaned fireplace and faced them. 'Simply that our staff has downed tools.'

'Downed tools?' Annette repeated, and saw the impatient frown Mrs. Revoir gave. 'I don't

162

understand.'

Mrs. Revoir spoke then, biting off her words sharply. 'Just that! The staff don't want to work for Valda. She has—shall we say?—an unfortunate approach.'

'They were lazy,' Valda said violently. 'Insolent.'

Henry gave a strange smile. 'So you keep telling us. However, they seem to have got their own back, for they are putting up a most successful passive resistance. They've all gone sick.'

Annette stared at him silently, frowning a little. She could not understand it. Rennie had always been so—

'They're shamming,' Valda said angrily.

Henry smiled coldly. 'I'm fully aware of that, Valda,' he said dryly, 'but short of getting a whip and beating them until they work as if they were my slaves, I don't see what can be done about it. The fact remains that life has become rather inconvenient. Rennie is carrying on gallantly with a very skeleton staff.'

'Rennie is the ringleader,' Valda said quickly. In her vividly striped frock, with her bright red hair, her blazing eyes, her red cheeks, she looked like a fury. 'You should sack the lot.'

'My dear Valda,' Henry said in an amused voice, 'it would appear that they have sacked us.'

There was silence while the two stared at

163

one another across the room, and then Henry said quietly, 'I can't help feeling, Valda, that somewhere you must have handled them wrongly. They are a proud people and not used to being treated like dogs.'

Valda's anger blazed again. 'I didn't treat them like dogs, but if I give an order I expect it to be carried out—and properly. They are slovenly, pampered—'

'Henri,' Annette said very quietly, afraid of what Valda would say next and hating the ugly scene. 'Perhaps they are ill. Perhaps it's an epidemic. Such a thing has never happened before. Madame Lascie said they were loyal—willing.' The air bristled with anger. 'If I see Rennie, consult—'

'Consult Rennie?' Valda seemed to explode. Like an angry rushing wind she crossed the room and flung open the door, staring angrily at Annette. 'Of course they'll come back *now*,' Valda said bitterly. 'Very clever of you, Annette,' she said, an angry scowl twisting her face into a new ugliness. 'But rather cheap—'

She flung the word at Annette and slammed the door behind her.

In the long silence that followed, Annette looked in bewilderment from Henry's amused face to Mrs. Revoir's bland smile. She saw, to her amazement, that the hostility had gone from Mrs. Revoir's eyes.

'I'm glad you're better, Annette,' Mrs. Revoir said, and rose. 'We have missed you.

164

Now I'll leave the lovebirds alone,' she added, and also left the room.

Her cheeks hot from that odd word, lovebirds, Annette turned appealingly to Henry, who had flung himself into an armchair and was lighting a cigarette.

'What did Valda mean? Clever of me?' she asked him.

His eyes were amused as he looked at her, his often stern face relaxed, his red hair rumpled as he thrust a hand through it. 'Just what she said. That it was clever of you to take to your bed and give her the chance to make a fool of herself.' He smiled at Annette's startled, horrified face. 'She hasn't a clue as to how to run a big house or handle staff. She looked a fool and not unnaturally resents it.'

There was dismay in Annette's candid eyes as her hand flew to her mouth. 'But, Henri, I didn't do it for that. It was just so heavenly to lie in bed, far from angry scenes and—' She stopped in distress, but he did not look cross, he merely looked as if he did not believe her. 'Henri,' she said earnestly, 'I swear I didn't do it for that. I wouldn't have humiliated Valda.' She paused. 'I couldn't run a house until Madame Lascie taught me.'

He flicked ash off his cigarette and smiled. 'I'm aware of that. All the same, Valda has always delighted in making others look fools, so it was quite amusing to see her made to look like one. It may do her good.' He stood

165

up and towered above her, smiling down almost tenderly. 'I don't want you to overdo things, Annette. You're very pale. I'll tell Rennie that you have recovered and that all is well. I must admit he looked after me very nicely.' Henry was on his way to the door, when he paused and chuckled. 'Do you know that even when we had eaten a meagre, badly-cooked meal, Rennie would bring me a tray of delicious food the instant I was alone?' He chuckled again. 'You know, Annette, the staff are wholeheartedly on your side.'

Suddenly she wanted to cry. She hated the thought of Valda feeling hurt and humiliated. 'There shouldn't be *sides*,' she said miserably, and then thought how childish it sounded.

Henry smiled. 'There shouldn't be lots of things,' he said, and left her to her thoughts.

In an incredibly short time, the staff had recovered and the Chateau buzzed with activity, soon to be shining like a new pin, even to fresh flowers in all the vases. Dinner was a beautifully cooked, well served and very restful meal, for Valda had asked for a tray to be sent to her room, and Mrs. Revoir was in a happy, friendly mood, telling Annette about her service flat in Regent's Park and that Henry must soon bring her over to England to visit her.

In the morning, clouds packed the sky and the sun could hardly be seen. A still heaviness still hung over the world and Annette escaped

166

to the garden and complimented Pierre, who straightened with some difficulty, on his flowers.

'I do not like the sky,' he said anxiously, gazing up at it. 'It is the season of the typhoons.'

Eager to get away from the Chateau and any possible scene with Valda, Annette rode to the convent where she was warmly welcomed by the Mother Superior, who had heard about her indisposition and was relieved to find she had recovered. 'Your wedding-dress is ready for a fitting,' she said, her pale cheeks flushed.

Ten minutes later Annette stared at her reflection in the mirror and found it hard to believe that the radiant girl with the eyes like stars could be herself. The wedding-dress was beautiful beyond words—made of beautiful lace, it had a fitting bodice with high neck and long sleeves, and a majestic skirt made of pleats to form a bustle and train.

'You are very lovely, my child,' the Mother Superior said softly, and her eyes shone with tears of affection. 'It is because of your happiness.'

Back at the Chateau, Annette ate a solitary lunch, for Henry had, it seemed, taken his mother out, and Valda was still eating in her bedroom. Annette, waited on by Rennie, could relax and let herself think that she was happy. Inadvertently she had defeated Valda.

167

In a little while she and Henri would be husband and wife, and Valda and Mrs. Revoir thousands of miles away, and life would really start.

As she drank coffee on the terrace, a small Creole child with a note arrived. It was from Jean.

'Meet me at your father's *campement* at three o'clock, please, Annette, for it is urgent. Jean.'

Wondering how it could be urgent, Annette was at the little house in good time The green parakeets came to screech rebukes at her as she disturbed them by entering the garden. There were gay flowers everywhere, the little house had been repainted, there were curtains at the windows, but no one lived there now.

She sat on the low wall of the veranda, gazing at the deep blue sea, for the sun chose that moment to come from behind a cloud, at the huge waves that raced towards the land. Feeling the familiar shock as the ground shook from the pummelling of the water, she looked at the distant mountains and thought of the short but happy time she had spent here with her father. How very glad she was that they had sent for her.

More screeching from the parakeets, and she saw that Jean Casca was walking towards her. He looked different—grave, unhappy—

perhaps even nervous, for he kept stroking his small dark moustache.

She was startled by his first words. 'Are you still afraid of Valda?' he asked.

Annette stared at him and her mouth went dry. 'Yes,' she whispered. And it was the truth. No matter what happened, she would always be afraid of Valda.

'You are a fool to fear that one,' Jean said angrily, his sallow skin turning dull red. 'She is dumb—she is without brains.'

Annette shivered. 'Jean ' She held out her hands vaguely as if searching for words, and the tall handsome Frenchman seized them. 'I think he still loves her,' she said quietly as she looked at him. All her newly found confidence vanished in that moment. How could she have thought so smugly that all was well? Had she forgotten that Henry loved Valda?

Jean held her hands against his chest and stared down into her small dismayed face. 'I love you—Annette,' he said hoarsely. 'You know that.'

She stared up at him in horror. 'Oh, no, Jean,' she cried quickly. 'I thought it was just a game with you.'

'Game?' he said bitterly. 'I have always loved you, Annette. Listen—in the morning I am to fly to Paris. There is awaiting me a very good position. I am in a dilemma, Annette. I do not wish to leave you if you need me, but—' His hands tightened on hers as he stared down

169

at her. 'I love you, Annette. Be my wife and fly with me to France.' As she stared at him in dismay, he said angrily, 'You will never find happiness with that cold man.'

Suddenly she wanted to cry because she had to hurt him. 'Oh, Jean—but I love him,' she said sadly.

'I know,' he began, and at that moment the green parakeets came swooping again, screeching noisily—and in the same moment, Annette had the fright of her life.

Roughly Jean pulled her into his arms, holding her tightly, forcing her head back as he kissed her with a wild passion that alarmed her.

Time seemed to stand still for a moment and then she found a strength she had not known she possessed. She broke free from his clutching arms and smacked his face.

Even as he stepped back, a red mark showing plainly on his cheek, an amused voice said, 'Well, well, Annette. Have you found you've bitten off more than you can chew for once?'

Annette swung round. Valda stood in the gateway, her hand linked loosely in Henry's arm. A Henry whose face was white and tense with anger as he strode forward.

Valda caught him by the arm, her laugh tinkling. 'Really, Henry—she's asked for it, the way she has encouraged him.'

Jean Casca had not moved. He stood, solid

as a rock, facing them all.

'Has she encouraged me?' he asked in a suddenly tired voice. 'I wish it was the truth.' He turned to Henry and gave a funny little bow. 'I have just requested Annette to become my wife and go with me to Paris. She has refused.' He turned to Annette, who was staring at him in dismay, unable to take her eyes from the red mark her hand had made. His voice softened. 'Forgive my roughness, *chèrie*. I would have preferred it another way, but because I love you, I had to prove something.' He drew a wad of bank notes from his pocket and, stepping forward, offered them to Valda.

'I am a man of honour,' Jean said slowly. 'Though you do not think so.' His voice was suddenly contemptuous. 'You tried to buy me. As you see, I did not earn the money.'

Valda made no move to take the money. She stood tense and still, her cheeks white, her eyes blazing. Jean Casca let the notes fall to the ground. He turned to Henry Revoir and bowed. 'You are a very fortunate man, *monsieur*. I wonder if you appreciate it,' he said, and with a last rueful smile at Annette, walked out of the gate and down the lane.

As the sound of his footsteps died away, Valda came to life. She bent to pick up the money and looked defiantly at Henry.

'All's fair in love,' she drawled.

'Only, in this case, it isn't love,' Henry said

in a strange flat voice.

Annette, shrinking against the wall, felt they had forgotten her as they stared at one another each breathing fast.

Valda took a step forward. 'She played a cheap trick on me,' she said, her slim body tensed.

Henry's smile was cold. 'The amusing part is, Valda, that she played no trick. She took to her bed because you made her so unhappy. You walked into a trap that had not been laid.'

Valda's eyes blazed for a moment. 'It's not true!' She stared at him and—horribly—her face seemed to crumple as she held out both hands. 'Henry,' she said softly. 'You can't marry her. You love—you love me.'

Annette, shivering, longed to move, but she could not. It was as she had thought. They loved one another. She had lost Henry—not that she had ever had . . . Not the real Henry.

'Yes, I loved you,' he was saying now, slowly. 'Until the day I woke and realized that you love only one person—and that is yourself, Valda.' Abruptly his voice changed, became cruelly cold, like ice. 'It's true, then. This was arranged for my benefit?'

'I wanted you to see the kind of girl she is,' Valda cried angrily.

It was shocking to hear him laugh. To hear him say almost affectionately, 'My poor Valda. Will you never learn that all girls are not like you? I saw the kind of girl Annette

172

is.' Again his voice changed, to the cruel cold tone that made Annette shiver. 'Valda—you will oblige me by returning immediately to the Chateau and remaining in your room. In the morning, I'll arrange for your immediate flight to England. Needless to say, I'll take care of expenses. We would prefer not to see you again,' he finished crisply.

He turned to Annette and saw her white scared face and he gently took her arm. 'Come, Annette, we must talk,' he said, and led her into the little house, turning the handle of the door as Annette had not thought of doing, closing the door on the white face of the angry Valda.

He took her into the little sitting-room. It was just as it had been in her father's lifetime, the furniture gleaming, the windows clean. Annette felt the tears well up in her eyes as she covered her face with her hands. This was the end, then. Now he would tell her he was sorry but he could not go through with the farce.

And then his arms were round her, cradling her, holding her close—comforting her, as he had comforted her when her father died.

'Don't cry, Annette,' he said gently, pulling her fingers from her face, gazing into the tragic, tear-stained eyes. 'I'm sorry you were forced to witness such an unpleasant scene, but it's over now.'

'I hit Jean so hard and—and it was only— only because he loved me,' Annette said, the tears starting again 'He startled me, Henri,' she said in a young ashamed voice. 'Never before had he done anything like that. I wish I hadn't hurt him so.'

'He understood,' Henry said quietly.

'And—and poor Valda,' Annette began again, and the wretched tears started afresh. 'Oh, Henri, she loves you. You can see it, and The unhappy words came with a rush. 'I know you love her.'

He sat down on the nearest chair and pulled her towards him, linking her in the circle of his arms, gazing steadily into her face.

'Listen, Annette, I stopped loving her a very long time ago,' he said very gently. 'I love you, Annette, I love you very much, but I'm always afraid to tell you because you fear me.'

Her tears were miraculously dried. She stared into his face and saw that he was not lying. 'But, Henri,' she began, and then her face brightened. 'Say that again!'

'I love you,' he said very slowly, smiling at her.

With a swift impulsive movement, she flung her arms round his neck and kissed him His arms tightened round her as he returned the kiss. At last he let her go and there was a strange look on his face.

'You're not afraid of me,' he said.

'I'm not afraid of you,' she told him, laughing a little. 'And I grew up the day I met you.' She leaned forward and did something

174

she had long wanted to do. She kissed the sweet silly little brown mole.

'I love you, Henri,' she said softly, and then, with another swift movement, she drew away from him, jerking off her engagement ring, thrusting it towards him, laughing a proud, excited little laugh as she saw the stricken look on his face, and saying very quickly, 'You put it on, Henri. You put it on. The last time you forgot.'

Her heart seemed to turn over as she saw the relief on his face. Did he love her so much? He slid the ring on her finger and cupped her face in his hands, kissing her gently on the mouth.

'You must forgive me, darling,' he said softly, 'but that was the first time in my life I had ever got engaged and I didn't know the correct procedure.'

'Oh, darling,' she said weakly as she leant against him and laid her mouth against his cheek. 'You must remember that this is the last time.'

She had so much to say to him, about her love and her fear, about Jacques le Roy and the mineral deposits, about their life together, but he caught her close and began to kiss her—and it seemed such a waste of time to talk when, instead, they could kiss.